ZANE

Pleasure Extraordinaire

Part 1

LIV BENNETT

Cover Model: Ryan Patrick
Photographer: Golden Czermak, FuriousFotog
Cover Designer: Sommer Stein, Perfect Pear Creative Covers

~

ZANE (Pleasure Extraordinaire: Part 1)

Zane Hawkins, the new CEO and the owner of Hawkins Media Group, is officially dating to marry. After two years of on-again-off-again romance with the actress Penelope Davis, Zane Hawkins is now ready to settle down. Multiple sources confirm that it's the recent death of his father causing him to re-think his bachelor lifestyle and consider starting a family of his own.

Who will be the lucky bride to tie down California's most eligible bachelor? A wildly famous Hollywood actress? An activist and visionary lawyer? A humble and media-shy nurse?

If the persisting rumors are true, there's a secret list of the most suitable candidates drawn up singlehandedly by Zane's very capable assistant, Julie Connor. Even so, Zane Hawkins has never been one to follow rules and directions.

Whoever is going to be the lucky winner, she deserves special kudos, as the road to Zane Hawkins' heart is known to go through several hoops and hurdles.

~

CH 1 - On the Road

"I can't be with you, Zane. I'm in love with your brother."

Her hair dark and wild, her lips red and swollen, she ¬wipes the tears away. Not hers, but mine. My fucking tears for wasting the opportunity to be with the one and only woman who could make me want to give up everything.

"No!" I scream as the silhouette of the woman who ripped my heart fades away into darkness, and suddenly my eyes ¬snap open. The nightmare quickly vanishes, and I feel sweat breaking out on my forehead.

How could I have been so stupid as to not realize she was the one, before my bastard brother and nemesis, Ace, snatched her from me?

I saw her first. I flirted with her first and she returned my advances. I fucked her first. But I didn't treat her like she deserved right from the beginning. That's where I lost the game. And that's why the nightmares about her declaring her love for my bastard brother wake me up in a sweat more often than I can handle.

I need a scotch. An entire bottle of the Glenlivet single malt pure goodness to numb my brain. It has been 158 goddamn days since I realized she's gone for good—158 days of torturous life that I've had to endure.

I scan the interior of the car I've been dozing off in and realize the car isn't moving. Pushing the button to lower the separator between me and my chauffeur, Daney, I ask him what the problem is.

"There seems to be a car accident at the Santa Monica and Wilshire crossing, sir," he replies, looking apologetic as if he caused the accident.

I exhale a long breath of frustration and glance down at my watch. Half an hour before my first appointment of the week. I'd better call Julie, my assistant, to reschedule it since the traffic doesn't seem to be moving anytime soon. A jolt of headache runs from my head down to my neck, making me wince with pain. The longer I sit here doing nothing, the more painful the headache will get. Restless and angry, I climb out of the car and text Julie to inform her of my impending tardiness.

As soon as I step out on the sidewalk, two young blonde girls giggle loudly and rush toward me. "Zane Hawkins!" they cheer in chorus, making a few heads turn with their high-pitched voices.

"Hi." I smile and glance down at my phone. I may not be a rock star or an A-list actor, but I get as much, or maybe even more attention from ladies as any big-name celebrity.

I'm the fucking owner and the chief executive of Hawkins Media Group that earned half a billion dollars in annual revenues just last year. I'm also the creator, producer, and occasional director of the top-rated and highly popular TV show, Frat House. My resume alone would get me laid on a daily basis even if I were a ninety-year-old dude with a breathing tube, saggy tits, and a wrinkly penis.

The two girls stand before me, too close for strangers to be, but I've never minded female attention, and today is no different. Both have long blonde hair down to their elbows, one curly and the other one straight as corn husk. The curly-haired one is wearing a short, pink summer dress which displays her long legs rather deliciously. The other girl has obviously skipped wearing a bra, and her nipples form beautiful buds beneath her low-cut blouse.

"I'm Beverly," the curly haired girl says eagerly. "And this is Teresa. We're big fans of Frat House. We know every line, every scene."

"Well, lucky you. I happen to have tickets for the shooting of the next episode." Putting my phone into the pocket of my dress pants, I grab my wallet from my other pocket and slip out the tickets.

Their eyes widen, and they start jumping up and down on the street, clapping their hands and screaming, "Oh, my God!" over and over again.

I smile as I hand them their tickets. "Don't forget to follow our Twitter and Facebook pages."

"We're already on both." Beverly snatches the tickets from my hand and throws herself at me, I assume, to show her gratitude.

I neither hug her back nor pull myself away from her enthusiastic embrace and just focus on the press of her ample boobs against my chest, as I let my eyes wonder over Teresa's breasts. Her nipples harden visibly, and as I move my gaze over her face and smile, I realize she's blushing, obviously aware of my intense study of her beautiful body.

They both look so young, I doubt they're legally adults. Their pussies must be used very little and tight as a glove. As delicious as they look and as much as I'd love to sink into their eager cunts, I'd rather not spend the rest of my life in prison as a sex offender for screwing underage kids.

I move away out of Beverly's hold slowly and nod my head at them. "I guess it's time for me to go." I glance down at my car and realize it hasn't moved an inch.

"No, don't go yet," Beverly calls out and grabs my hand. "The traffic will take a while."

"Yeah, it will. Why don't you get us a room at the Nouvelle Suites and chill with us rather than wasting your time in your car?" Teresa asks and motions with her chin toward the Nouvelle Suites hotel right behind us.

"Yeah, we'll make it worth your time. I promise," Beverly adds eagerly.

"Well, I'm not sure." I scratch the back of my head, studying the luscious bodies of both girls.

They're both fair-skinned and slim, except for their perky breasts and relatively toned hips. Teresa's stomach is flat beneath her blouse and makes me want to lick all over her smooth skin until I dip my tongue into her pussy.

My cock stirs with the thoughts of enjoying two innocent-looking girls. A sweaty fucking session is definitely a better way to start the day than a glass of scotch, but there's still the problem with their ages. "How old are you?"

"Oh, don't worry about that. We're both

nineteen." Teresa quickly produces her driver's license and hands it to me. Beverly follows suit. Their ages check out, which means there's no obstacle between my cock and their pussies.

A sane man would worry about the potential dangers of picking up random girls off the street to have sex with, a possible kidnapping and blackmail scenario among the first and perhaps the deadliest, but who said I was a sane man? "All right, then. You, go ahead and wait for me in the lobby. I'll be a minute."

They nod their heads in response and start running down the street, which gives me a chance to check out their asses. Both nice and firm. This is going to be fun.

After ordering Daney to drive to the parking lot of the hotel, I head for the reception desk and hand my credit card to the middle-aged, brunette receptionist. She smiles at me in recognition and quickly reserves a suite for me, and all the while I wonder if I should add her to my little morning play.

She makes sure our hands touch as she

gives me my card back, and I wink at her along with a playful smile, but dismiss the idea of having her in order to spare myself the trouble of having to explain to her about Teresa and Beverly.

"Have a great day," the receptionist wishes me as I turn toward the elevators and spot my giggling girls.

"He's so hot." I hear Teresa whisper, and Beverly nods her head several times, her chest moving up and down way too quickly.

I place my hands at the small of their backs and guide them toward the elevator under the curious eyes of the other hotel guests. As soon as the elevator doors close on us, Teresa wraps her arms around me and pushes her lips against mine. While exploring her mouth, I feel Beverly rubbing her body against the side of my body, her hands immediately landing on my growing erection.

These girls are nothing but innocent, and I have no complaints whatsoever about it.

We practically run to my suite, and while I slide the keycard to open the door, Teresa starts unbuttoning her blouse, her eyes locked on my face, her bottom lip between her teeth. My phone buzzes as I open the door. The girls walk into the bedroom, and I glance down at the screen of my phone to see Julie's calling.

Declining the call and turning off the phone, I slide out of my jacket and watch as the girls slowly undress before me. Teresa's blouse lands on the floor first. Her breasts are big and firm, better than I'd imagined, her nipples are hard and require my immediate attention.

Beverly quickly makes up for lost time and pulls her dress over her head, standing in a light-pink bra and a tiny triangle of a thong before me.

I go for Teresa, nonetheless, and unbutton and unzip her jeans and quickly slip my hand beneath her panties to feel her soaking pussy. She moans while I slide my finger between her pussy lips.

Beverly mirrors my behavior and works on the zipper of my pants, pushing them down along with my boxer briefs. My cock springs free in full size, ready to fuck the brains out of these two girls.

While Teresa rides my hand to her first

orgasm in loud moans, Beverly kneels in front of me and parts her plump red lips, looking impatient to prove her oral skills.

Teresa's pussy vibrates around my fingers, and Beverly quickly mouths my cock to its base, gagging as my cock hits the depths of her throat.

Teresa might have the bigger breasts and better body, but it's Beverly that now has my full focus thanks to her eager sucking. I drop Teresa and run my hands through Beverly's thick curls to hold her in place while I pump hard into her mouth. She's unquestionably an expert at cocksucking and reminds me of the only other excellent cocksucker I know of—Lindsay.

Fuck! I shouldn't go there. Not now. Not ever.

Angry at myself for letting thoughts of Lindsay get into my head, I push Beverly's head back and release myself from her mouth. She falls on her butt and looks up at me in shock and hesitation.

"Get on your feet and bend down in front of the bed. Both of you," I order.

Both girls get out of the last pieces of

clothing, walk fully naked toward the bed, and, as ordered, line up at the end of it and bend down, displaying their firm asses and swollen, pink pussies to me. Their breasts hang down, their skin and hair glowing under the dim light flowing through the curtains.

Grabbing two condoms out of my wallet, I sheath my cock with one and position myself behind Teresa. My eyes trail the crevice between her ass cheeks down to the pulsating folds of her pussy and her glistening juices. I land my hands on each cheek and spread them apart, watching the muscles around her back opening clench in response.

"Have you ever been fucked in the ass?" I ask.

"No," Teresa replies.

"I have." Beverly interferes with my interaction with Teresa, looking at me over her shoulder. "I love anal."

I give her an appreciative smile and push the head of my cock into Teresa's pussy. She's as tight as I've imagined, and the evidence of her arousal lubes my condom-clad cock generously. Her hands fall on the edge of the bed as I pump into her, harder with each second. Even Beverly's jealous glare can't stop her from moaning in pleasure, and soon her pussy starts pulsating with wild quivers.

Smiling in satisfaction, I push myself out of Teresa and slip the used condom off and roll on a new one for Beverly. She lets out a squeak of excitement and pulls her legs together, pushing her hips higher in the air, ready to catch my cock.

"I don't carry lube with me," I say.

"That's okay. I'm wet enough in my pussy," Beverly explains between her ragged breaths.

I run a finger between the lips of her pussy to check, although her glistening juices can be detected a mile away.

Pushing the lips of her sex aside with my fingers, I ease into her opening and listen to her exaggerated moans as I inch deeper inside her. She's tighter than Teresa, which makes me curious as to how much tighter she'll be in the ass. After two strokes, I slip out and push the head of my cock against her ass opening, glancing at Teresa briefly while she's now lying on her back on the bed, her hands playing with her breasts. She's clearly aware of the beauty of those firm globes and uses it to her advantage to steal my attention from her friend.

Girls and the competition between them...makes for an incredible sexual adventure.

As much as I enjoy watching Teresa, my eyes land back on Beverly's ass so I won't hurt her butt in the process. True to her words, Beverly opens up for me, and I ease into her with only a slight protest of her tight muscles. I'm a goner for anal, and her eagerness to have me inside her ass, puts her ahead of the game.

That and her loud moans. I'd consider taking her as my lover if I hadn't been already dealing with a couple of dozen.

The tightness of her ass around my shaft makes it hard for me to prolong my erection, but I owe her at least an orgasm for offering her ass to me, not to mention that Teresa got two. Moving my hand down, I press my fingers against Beverly's clit and rub it first gently then intensify the pressure. In a matter seconds, she climaxes in my hand, her even louder moans echoing against the four walls of the large suite.

I hear Teresa chuckling while my eyes close, my own climax only a few pumps away. Holding Beverly's hips with both hands, I thrust harder into her and explode inside the condom, feeling my heart beating against my ears.

As soon as the last drip of sperm is out, my attraction to the two girls hits bottom, and a feeling of disgust surfaces. I slip out of Beverly and walk to the trash can, get the condom off and throw it into the can.

I consider hopping into the bathtub for a quick shower, but the girls look eager not to leave it with only one round, and I'd rather not fuck someone whose name I'll forget in an hour, for a second time, so I only wash my hands and hurry to put on my clothes.

"Enjoy the suite for the day and order whatever you want. It's on me," I say as I walk toward the door without even looking back to see what they're up to. I hear them saying goodbye and close the door.

Twenty minutes of fun with two beautiful girls without any strings attached. That's exactly how a satisfying sexual encounter should be, except for the feeling of disgust that's ruining my good mood. I didn't have it before Lindsay. Gone are the days I used to just feel good and carry on with my daily life after a good round of sex.

I guess it's the curse of falling in love with the wrong woman...or falling in love altogether.

CH 2 - On the Market

Julie stands as I enter her office. She's not just my secretary but also my long-time accomplice in my successful effort to rid myself of my father and take over the reins of Hawkins Media Group. Clad in a long, black skirt-suit, she holds her black cup of coffee in her hand, her eyebrows tightly pulled together into an angry furrow.

I don't remember the last time she had a different color on, perhaps before my mother's death more than a decade ago? But at that time, I didn't care enough about her to even notice what she was wearing. Over the years she's become such a big part of my professional and private life, she's practically irreplaceable. Hawkins Media Group could survive without me running it, but without Julie, it wouldn't even make it a full year.

"I'd really appreciate it if you didn't decline my calls," she says in her usual feverish way. "Brad had an urgent matter to discuss with you about the next episode's scenario. Apparently, one of the writers went into labor last night, and we need to find a replacement for her very quickly." She doesn't sound pleased by my rudely declining her calls; obviously, but there's something else, something out of the ordinary beneath her anger.

My eyes traveling over her face up to the tight bun on the top of her head, I slip my hands into the pockets of my pants. "What about the other writers on the team? Ask them to work overtime to compensate for the lost hours. They won't be the first team to work a few extra hours in the entertainment industry." The only reason I'm yelling at her, rather than speaking softly is because she's one of the few women I know, who won't collapse on their desk in tears, but rather push my buttons for a heated discussion.

And, as expected, she narrows her eyes at

me in an angrier fashion, sizing me up and down, although clearly, I'm her boss, and my power is absolute. "You're probably not aware of the tiny little fact that they're already working a hundred hours a week and not getting paid for their extra work."

"Well, then pay them for the extra hours so they'll shut up and do their work properly."

"Sir, with all due respect, I seriously think we need to hire one or two more writers. With their workload, the current writers will burn out very soon, and we'll lose the momentum of the series. I have already identified three candidates and can schedule an interview with them for this afternoon." She grabs a file from her desk and extends it to me.

Smiling, I shake my head, ignoring the file she's holding before my face. "Since when do you call me sir?"

Her cheeks blush, perhaps for the first time in the seventeen years that I've known her, making my grin grow wider. "Zane," she corrects her mistake and adds, "You should really take a look at the profiles of the candidates and interview them as soon as possible."

"Nah. I'll pass. You interview them."

Her eyebrows raise in excitement; her lips part in surprise. "Really?"

"Come on! You've been my right arm through thick and thin against my father. You can manage a dull interview now, can't you?"

"Of course, I can. I just didn't think you'd trust me with those issues."

I smirk and walk toward my office door. "You clearly don't know how much I trust you. I could practically leave the entire corporation to you, and I have no doubt you'd run it as well as I do." Perhaps even better, but she doesn't need to know that.

Looking over my shoulder as I open the door to my office, I see her smile in confidence. "Can you get me a cup of coffee?"

Her good mood sours visibly as she looks at me with a disappointed expression.

I laugh. "Just kidding. I'll drink scotch. Want to join me?"

"Zane, please don't do that. With the amount of alcohol you're consuming, you're going to end up becoming an alcoholic. Don't do it to yourself." She plops into her chair when I walk into my office without responding to her worry-filled warning.

Of course, she's right, but I have yet to figure out any other way to get over the pain. So I drink to make it go away...even if it works only for a moment.

Confused about how I'll pass the morning without liqueur clouding my mind, I settle on my chair and notice the pile of magazines I'm sure Julie set out for me. Picking up one, I study the cover featuring a picture of Penelope and me on it.

"Zane Hawkins, the CEO and the owner of Hawkins Media Group, is officially dating to marry," says the title of the LA Celebrity News magazine.

Rolling my eyes at the utter craziness of the possibility of me marrying, I flip through the pages and find the article to read it to see what bullshit the creative journalist came up with about me this time.

After two years of on-again-off-again romance with the actress Penelope Davis, Zane Hawkins is now ready to settle down. Multiple sources confirm that it's the recent death of his father, Michael Hawkins, that made him re-think his bachelor lifestyle and consider starting a family of his own.

I chuckle, despite the irritation I get every time I'm reminded of my father, and call out for Julie.

"Have you read this bullshit?" I ask although I have no doubt she has not only read and memorized each line written about me in the media, but also carefully reviewed the piece for its appropriateness before its publication. She's a perfectionist when it comes to her job, but one of her best qualities is she never leaves a misbehaving journalist or blogger unpunished. I think she gets extra satisfaction from having the company attorney send out cease-and-desist orders almost as much as she enjoys bothering me.

Still holding her cup of coffee, she steps into my office and slides elegantly into the chair before my desk, her face brightly lit with a sly smile "Bullshit? You're breaking my heart. What's bullshit about it?"

"Everything. None of it is true."

"Oh. Would you have rather it said 'after his recent failure to win the heart of the girl he loved and consequently losing her to his brother, Zane is fucking everything with a hole to mend his broken heart?'"

I chuckle to keep my cool and also to show her I'm not affected by her words, although they're nothing but the truth. "I should have never told you anything about Lindsay." Even voicing her name tightens my chest in pain, and the thought of the loving looks she gives to Ace floods through my mind.

Julie's smile gives way to a warm, yet sad, expression. "You didn't need to tell me—I knew it before you even realized you were falling for her."

"Really?" Can't a man have a few secrets to himself?

She nods and sips her coffee.

I pick another random magazine from among the pile of nonsense and read the title on the cover. "Five Things Zane Hawkins is Looking for in a Wife." I read it out loud and lift my gaze to her, trying my best not to laugh at the ridiculousness of the title. "Do you know the five things I'm looking for in a wife, too?"

She covers her mouth with a hand while chuckling. "That was just to increase the ratings of Frat House, and I admit, it was a lot of fun coming up with the bullet points."

I scan the article before me, shaking my head at the complete absurdity of each point that supposedly represents my requirements for a woman who would carry my name. "She should be able to cook and bake. Really? That's the number one requirement? Not fantastic oral skills or possession of a great booty?"

She rolls her eyes at me disapprovingly. "Great oral skills or some fat ass won't feed your children. And please don't tell me you have the iron chef cooking your meals for you. Nothing beats food cooked with love. Would you want your future kids to eat food cooked by their mom or by some restaurant chef?"

Without commenting on her valid argument, I proceed to the second point in the article. "She should believe in God. That can't be real. I don't even remember the last time I went to church."

"During your mother's funeral," she

reminds me and adds. "I didn't come up with this one, I promise. It was your mom's idea."

"My mom's? My dead mom's idea?"

"Yeah, well. She made me promise her a variety of things before...you know...she took her own life. And one of the promises was that I'd help you find a truly God-fearing woman for a wife."

"What else did she make you promise?"

She bites her lower lip. "I'd rather not say."

Any conversation regarding my mother and her death by suicide is off limits, which is why I continue with the article rather than pushing Julie to spill her secrets. "Unselfish, undemanding and independent. Finally something I'd value in a woman."

"I'm glad I could get you to agree on at least one point."

"She should be one hundred percent loyal to me. This one is absolutely true, but it should actually be the number one requirement. She should be loyal to me as a man and as a partner in life."

Julie's lips curl up and part in a broad smile, contentment and pride apparent in her face. "Gosh, I so knew you'd say that." She stands, walking around my desk, and stops next to me, glancing down at the magazine in my hands.

I freeze for a moment as the scent of her perfume hits me. Honeysuckle.

Her perfume is the only feminine quality she has, and each time I get to smell it, my body stills momentarily and I'm reminded of the fact that she's not just some employee or a good friend, but also a woman with breasts and a vagina beneath her unflattering clothes.

"Why don't you for once wear something sexy?" I ask, completely forgetting about the context of my relationship with her.

Her face turns sad in an instant, and her eyes fall on the desk. "You wouldn't ask me that question if you knew about the things your father forced me to do."

My whole body tenses, my hands ball into fists, and I want to hit myself for reminding her of the evil things my father did to her. I'm well aware of the things she had to go through as my father's assistant for all those years, but I have no idea why she's stayed for so long. Was that also a part of her promise to my mother?

"I'm very sorry." I turn my head down to the magazine to change the subject and hopefully to make her forget about the painful past. "Be sexually open-minded," I read the last item and laugh. "That's my girl!" I shout with an extra note of cheerfulness to distract her. "You indeed know me well."

"You work as a gigolo at Pleasure Extraordinaire. I figured you'd be a total waste of time for a virgin or a prude."

Ah yes, my part-time work at the brothel that caters to sweet, sexual and extremely horny women from all around the country. The place that widens my horizons about women. Not just fashion models or movie actresses, but I get to enjoy a large variety of women, anything from bored housewives and CEO's to cougars, Latinas...you name it.

Prostitutes can get me only so far, and I've always been suspicious of the random women who throw themselves at me. They aren't that different from prostitutes, at least most of them. Who knows if it's me and my body that get their panties wet or the inheritance I received from my father, or the doors they hope I might open for them—the doors to the big screen, perhaps?

That paranoia of mine dissolves into thin air the moment I step into the magical world of Pleasure Extraordinaire which is filled with delightful surprises. The women I get to know there never disappoint, neither with their intentions to go under me, nor with their high performance. I can't wait to indulge myself in one soon.

Julie draws in a long breath of air and lands her eyes on me, still looking bothered. "Now that you know you're officially looking for a wife to marry, I'll set up a list of appropriate women for you to date, but feel free to let me know if you have someone special in mind that you want to get to know." She pauses and locks her eyes on mine, looking as if she's expecting me to come up with a name this instant.

"Ahhh," I mumble, still trying to soak in the idea of marriage. "I don't think it's a good idea. Realistically speaking, I won't marry, and even if I do by some miracle, I'm not born to be a monogamous man. I love women as in plural."

"No man is born to be monogamous. It's what you choose to become for the woman you love and the family you will form. Look, you're pushing thirty-three. The quality of your sperm is diminishing each passing day, and you're wasting your good sperm on flings and one-night stands, rather than making babies and continuing your legacy."

"Excuse me! My sperm is in perfect shape," I correct her, rather insulted by her insinuation. No one has the right to offend my manhood, not even Julie.

She exhales loudly as if trying to keep herself from arguing with my statement. "I promised your mother I'd take care of Chloe, Ace, and you. Both Chloe and Ace have found their partners and neither need my help anymore. You're the only burden on my shoulders. You have to find a wife and start a family so I can complete my mission and start my own life. I'm tired of babysitting you."

"I don't need you taking care of me. I'm a grown man in case you haven't noticed."

"I don't care." She takes a step closer to

me, her eyebrows pulled together, her eyes narrowed. "Irene was one of the very few people who positively impacted my life and I won't turn my back on her by breaking my promise. You'll find an appropriate woman and marry her by the end of the year, even better if you can knock her up within the first few months of your marriage..." She lifts her hand and points her index finger at me "...or so help me I'll ruin your reputation so badly no woman will ever want to so much as touch you."

"Spare your energy. Nothing you can say or do will convince me." I push my chair back with my feet to keep a safe distance between us.

"Oh, yeah? How about this? Thirty years from now. You will be sixty-two and won't be in the best shape to run a billion-dollar company. Who do you think will take over control? Who will be the next owner and CEO of Hawkins Media Group? Let me answer it for you. One of Ace's children. Is that what you what? You lost the woman you loved to Ace. Do you really want to lose the legacy of HMG to his offspring as well? Think about it for a moment."

She might be right. I never wanted him to be part of my family, and I'll do everything I can to keep his children from taking over the company my own father founded. I might have hated Michael for a variety of reasons, but I won't deny his hard work and the sacrifices he made to make the company what it is today.

I let out a long breath of defeat and shrug my acceptance. Julie is right. I need a beautiful, sexy and honorable woman to bear and raise my children, and I need her now!

Julie's angry face turns into a scary kind of happy in a heartbeat. "Good! I'll email you the list."

CH 3 - On the Edge

The smile of disbelief remains on my lips long after Julie returns to her desk.

Me, married?

Taking care of a family and tiny human beings?

I snort. It doesn't sound like something a man with my money and killer looks should take upon himself. I'd rather have one of my previous lovers show up with a child of mine and claim child support than have to go through the ordeal of being a husband. That would seriously be a last-ditch attempt to secure the future of my company.

However, in all honesty, the women I've slept with aren't exactly mother-quality and would raise a child in less than stellar conditions. I don't claim to have the potential to become a great father, but I have the resources, a.k.a. money, to have them raised in qualified hands and send them to the best schools.

I find myself agreeing with the qualities Julie came up with for the woman who'd mother my child, or perhaps children, mentally adding the requirement that the passion continue. But she's a fool if she thinks I'll seriously consider personally putting myself in the prison of monogamy and exclusivity. I might as well move into federal prison.

Longingly, I eye the bottles of liquor lined up neatly on the coffee table in the seating area in the corner. If I'll indeed be a father, alcohol shouldn't have a place in my life, or at least not as much of one as it's had these past months.

I phone Daney and ask him to take care of the bottles for me. He nods when he enters my office carrying an empty cardboard box and quickly starts loading the three bottles of alcohol on the coffee table and another half-dozen in the liquor cabinet.

Julie reminds me of my lunch appointment with Brad, the director of the Frat House show. I'd skip it and ask her to postpone it if it wasn't already his third attempt to meet with me.

"All right. I'm on my way." I grab my phone and head out once Daney has all the alcohol safely packed in the box and places it in Julie's capable hands.

She smiles as she murmurs something devious into her earpiece mic, her face brightening up as her sinister grin widens. She's onto something, and I'm afraid I'll find out what it is very soon.

Brad has been the director of Frat House since day one, although he allows me to take control of a few episodes if only for publicity reasons.

We meet at the set. I take a few minutes to chat with the actors and the cast to listen to the latest issues and problems they encounter during the shootings. I guess having the boss of all the bosses before you psychologically turns them into happy campers, because none of them, even the four main actors can't bring themselves to point out any issues related to their work, which is another reason why I need Julie. She's a smooth operator and people trust her with their complaints without worrying about getting fired.

After my failed attempt at getting my people to talk about work-related problems, I head directly to Brad's office and find him talking with Scarlett, the actress who plays the female lead of Frat House. Her eyes widen when she notices me, her thin eyebrows raising on her forehead. Quickly, she gets to her feet and shakes hands with me. Her face is all soft and smiley, her cheeks blushing an adorable shade of pink, as we exchange pleasantries.

Scarlett is probably the only person who is sincere about her interest in her colleagues. She listens, and she cares deeply. I've never seen her yelling at a makeup artist or even frowning at the employees beneath her pay grade. She's 5"8' tall, has long blonde hair and unusually light green eyes, just like the character Brad and I had in mind when we first discussed the series. But I'd pick her for the role even if her looks didn't match.

She has a strong character, unyielding and achievement oriented, likely as a result of being raised as the only girl and the youngest of the eight kids in an impoverished farm family in Ohio. Her parents didn't want her to go to high school and instead kept her on the farm, but she taught herself Spanish, literature, and math, with books and CDs she borrowed from the local library. She got accepted to the college of nursing at Ohio State where I auditioned her for the role.

Her raw beauty and the assured way she carried herself despite her young age were the first qualities I noticed about her, but her brilliant mind and resilience made me decide on the spot she was the one and that she wouldn't disappoint. She was like a mature and smart forty-year-old woman wrapped up in an eighteen-year-old body.

Even after four seasons into the series, she's still the first one to show up on the set and the only one who always delivers her lines correctly on the first go. She's superb in every sense.

"Hey, Zane. Is it true you're hunting for a wife?" She slides her arm through mine as we walk toward the chairs in Brad's office.

I laugh and pull out a chair for her. She thanks me briefly, her eyes locked on mine with a childish happiness sparkling in them. I wish Chloe, my sister, had half the sympathy and compassion Scarlett has. To Chloe, everyone wants something from her and no one is to be trusted. I don't blame her for becoming paranoid, though. No one who grew up under my father's abuse could have become a healthy and happy individual.

"When do you find time to read tabloids?" I ask.

"I read everything about you. So, do you want me to fix you up with one of my friends?"

"You might not have noticed but I'm thirty-two. You know what they'll call me if I start dating a twenty-year-old?" I pause to wait for her answer, but she only shakes her head with curiosity. "A creeper. I don't want to give anyone a reason to call me that. At least not before I turn fifty." I laugh.

"I bet you'll be a hot piece of ass as a fifty-year-old," she says and turns to Brad. "Don't you think, Brad?"

Brad winces, as if he's been offered food right out of a dumpster and pulls a blue folder out of his drawer. "We have more pressing issues to talk about than Zane's ass in his fifties. If you don't mind?" He lifts a hand in the air and waves it as a gesture to dismiss her while his face still looks cringed.

"Sorry. I gotta go." Scarlett stands quickly and grips my shoulder in a gentle squeeze. "Zane."

"Scarlett."

I crane my head to watch her out and as soon as she closes the door, I turn back to Brad with a murderous glare. "What gives you right to treat her like a piece of shit?"

Brad's hand holding the blue folder remains frozen in the air while he looks at me with a shocked expression. "I'm sorry, Zane. I didn't mean anything."

"For you, it's Mr. Hawkins from now on. Your behavior is unacceptable. Next time, remind yourself that if I ever have to choose between her and you, it's you who'll be out the door. She's irreplaceable, but you are not."

"It wasn't my intention to be

disrespectful. Scarlett and I are good friends. She knows I could never be mean to her," he defends himself, his voice almost cracking as if he'll start crying in a second.

"Whatever." I spread my legs and slip my phone out of my pocket. "What did you want to talk about?" I ask, glancing down at my phone to deprive him of my attention. He's not respectful to his subordinates; he doesn't deserve my full attention. He basically repeats the same thing Julie was lecturing me about, that being, how behind the writer team is on the script and whatnot. I nod without speaking and only at the end, do I tell him the issue is being taken care of.

He stands and walks me out, apologizing one more time as he opens the car door for me. I call Julie to cancel my afternoon appointments and order Daney to take me to Pleasure Extraordinaire to let off steam.

On the ride, I log into my Pleasure Extraordinaire account and skim through the ladies who are up for a little afternoon gymnastics. A new client asks for an all-nighter fuck fest and has a few juicy photos of her tight, petite body posted to lure in the gigolos of Pleasure Extraordinaire, but so far, no one's taken an interest in her.

I wouldn't be the gentleman I am today if I didn't help out a woman in need of a big, hard cock, so I volunteer and send her a few pictures from my private gallery for her to decide. Her confirmation message comes in quickly along with more photos of her, specifically her pussy. I love me a woman who doesn't shy away from sending pussy pics. I devour each image from several angles, feeling my cock getting hard in preparation for tonight's fuck fest.

"Have a great afternoon, sir." Daney nods as I get out of the car.

"I'll stay the night. Come pick me up tomorrow at six," I order and head off to the tall gates of the mighty Pleasure Extraordinaire mansion.

A group of boys, whom we call mannequins, are lined up on each side of the hall, which means a client is coming. They're wannabe gigolos whose only job is to stand half-naked at the entrance hall all day long to welcome guests. Their muscles are bulging beneath their solarium-tanned skins, but that's all there is to them.

I don't see any of them becoming a wanted gigolo like me or JJ Triple X, whose fame is larger than the state of California or any other permanent gigolos of Pleasure Extraordinaire. It takes an unbeatable level of self-confidence, years of sexual experience, and also money, to turn on the type of women who are customers here, and only a few men can score high in all categories.

To sign in, I walk straight to the office of the director, who also happens to be my adopted brother, Ace. Having to endure his face, his whole demeanor, is the only downside of this job, and of course, the fact that he's the one who got Lindsay.

I knock on the door of his office and listen. I know for a fact Lindsay is right now at her cubicle at Hawkins Media Group, but still, I can't help but fear I'll hear her moans of pleasure behind the door of Ace's office.

Fortunately, he's alone in his office and barely lifts his head to acknowledge my presence as I enter.

I sink into a chair before his desk. "Looks like I'm in demand for tonight."

"The client wants someone for twenty-four hours," he states, keeping up his efforts of not sparing me a glance.

"I'll clear my schedule for tomorrow if that's what she wants." I'm all for an enthusiastic, energetic lady who's down for a several hours of fuck session.

"Good. Did you have sex within the last twenty-four hours?" he asks with a less-than-enthusiastic tone of voice.

"Yeah, why?"

"Why?" At last, he lifts his head and fixes his angry eyes on me. "If you're to serve a client for a full day, you should abstain from sex for at least that much time. That's in the Pleasure Extraordinaire 101 booklet that everyone, including you, should have memorized by heart."

"So what if I fucked a few hours ago. I can handle a day or two of fucking without any problems."

"I don't care what mythical superhero you think yourself to be. Customer satisfaction is my main concern. I'd rather turn down a client than offer her used-up goods."

I laugh as hard and loudly as I can. Used-up goods? Is he still holding a grudge for me having my way with Lindsay? Apparently, yes.

He doesn't blink an eye as he watches my laughter fade away. "Request her for a reschedule. If she doesn't accept it, I'll ask around for someone else to fill in for you."

"No, don't do that. She wants me. Asked for me specifically."

"Goodness gracious. Get over yourself, Zane. She doesn't even know who you are."

I roll my eyes at his unusually annoying attitude. Something is up, and I have a suspicion it's not sunny in paradise anymore. "Why so grumpy, little brother? Aren't you getting any at home?" I grunt.

"Fuck you! Get out of my office," he yells at me. His nostrils flare while his face turns red instantly.

I purse my lips together to resist my urge to laugh or make another joke. I need to get laid. The quicker, the better, and I kind of like it here at Pleasure Extraordinaire, so I should at least play my part as his subordinate to not get kicked out. "Sorry. I'm taking back my joke. I swear I'll give the client an unforgettable night. Have I ever disappointed a client? No. Have I always been honest with you about my sexual habits? Again no. But, I'll give the client what she wants and more. I swear I will. She'll leave the mansion as a happy, swooning, and well-fucked woman. Satisfaction guaranteed or her money will be fully refunded."

He gives his head a one-time shake, and I know that's it for the discussion. I can perform a somersault in the air, and he won't change his mind. It was easier to handle him when Michael was around. Now that he's gone, I can't bring up Michael to convince him to comply with my wishes.

"God, Ace. Whatever. You'll have to deal with the client's disappointment for not having my dick tonight." I start to stand and head for the door, but someone opens it ever so slowly. My eyes grow large in satisfaction, as I start studying the blonde hottie who smiles at me and steps into the office.

"Hi!" Her voice comes out squeaky as she darts her eyes between Ace and me, then her jaw drops. "Oh, my God. Zane Hawkins! Is that you? Don't tell me you work here."

I give her my million-dollar grin along with a flirty wink as I hold out my hand to shake. "McKenzie Richmond. Must be my lucky day. I'm finally graced with the honor to make your acquaintance." Gripping her hand, I lift it up to my lips and watch her squirm and blush with the brush of my lips on the tender skin of her knuckles.

McKenzie is the one and only daughter of four-time-Grammy-Award-winning singer, Levi Richmond. Just like her father, McKenzie has made a name for herself with her wild parties, drug consumption, and, of course, her sexual adventures with multiple lovers. It was only a matter of time until she found her way to Pleasure Extraordinaire to satisfy her wild urges.

Her youthfulness and energy shine through the strapless, red super mini-dress that's tightly hugging her lean body. She must be on a strict diet of champagne and meth to keep her skinny looks. Bless the heart of the plastic surgeon who upgraded her boobs, because they're large and perky without the support of a bra.

Flicking her long hair over her shoulder, she sizes me up from head to toe without any attempt to hide her obvious assessment and smiles, a sign she's appreciative of what she sees. Her tongue brushes her lipstick coated lips.

She slips her hand out of my hold and walks toward Ace's desk. "I assume you're Ace Hawkins."

I cover my mouth casually to hold back a laugh. My poor brother is the only Hawkins whose face doesn't get instant recognition. And rightly so, because he's not a real Hawkins.

Ace welcomes her curtly and glances at the screen on his desk to retrieve McKenzie's application data. "It usually takes a few weeks to process the application for a new client, but due to your circumstances and medical records proving the lack of STD's, we can expedite your application and reserve you an afternoon or a night with one of my employees."

I'm curious about her special circumstances, but it's not my place to ask. I'm here only to give pleasure without any questions or prejudices. Another question that begs an immediate answer is why she's here. She's young, beautiful and independently wealthy. And as far as I know she doesn't have a husband or a fiancé to hide her sexual adventures from. Aside from her need to be fucked well, I don't see why she should be paying money to get sex.

"I heard great things about JJ," she says, grinning and gives me a sideway glance. "But, now I'm undecided."

"You can have them both, simultaneously or at different times, as long as they're onboard with your wishes," Ace explains.

I don't think JJ will decline her as long as she satisfies his need for money. He claims he doesn't care about money, but he charges the most. And, he lives here and never eats out. I haven't seen him even ordering pizza from outside. For all I know, every cent he's earning goes right into his bank account.

"Simultaneously, of course," McKenzie chirps with extra excitement and leans against the desk, pointing her index finger toward Ace's face. "And, I want you in the mix, too."

Ace stills for a moment, a shadow of insult crossing on his face. "Thanks for your interest, but I don't play."

"Oh, that's unfair. You shouldn't look so damn sexy." McKenzie pouts and leans forward, possibly in an effort to showcase her wide chest.

Ace blinks a few times, looking discomfited by the abundance generously displayed right before his nose. "I'm sorry."

I laugh and move forward to stand beside McKenzie to direct her attention back to me. "His girlfriend has a tight leash on him if you know what I mean."

McKenzie laughs loudly at my joke and turns her body toward me, running her gaze from my chest down to my crotch. God, this girl has no shame.

"I don't like being turned down." Stepping closer to me, she circles her long fingers around my tie, pulling it and me against her body. "How about just watching without playing?" She cranes her head to glance at Ace, her expression expectant. "Please!"

"You'll watch it anyway through the

surveillance cameras. Why not allow her to play in your office?" I ask to convince Ace and to finally start the action. My cock is already semi-hard and wants to get wet inside a tight hole, preferably McKenzie's eager pussy.

Ace glares at me, looking angry as if he's trying hard not to burst out at me. The door opens after a quick knock on it, and JJ enters, as always without wearing anything above the waist. That, too, must be one of his tricks to save money.

"Well, hello!" JJ walks directly toward McKenzie without paying any attention to Ace or me, grabs her hand and pulls her, not so gently, against his muscled body.

McKenzie reacts only with a soft whimper and throws her body into his arms, hugging him as if they're old friends.

"Oh, my. Are you for real?" She stares at him for long moments, rubbing her lips against each other with a hint of hunger. Only cougars who have been abandoned for several years show their craving for male attention so obviously. This girl must have real daddy issues to be behaving so sexually. "I want all three of you! I don't care about the money. I'll pay whatever it takes."

"I can't." Ace insists, the kill-joy.

"Not even for watching?" she asks. She's as adamant as Ace. I'm very close to reminding Ace of his earlier talk about customer satisfaction.

Without waiting for Ace's answer, McKenzie pulls JJ's head down and plasters her lips against his, and for me, she rolls the hem of her dress up to her waist to show me her bare ass.

No panties.

I should have guessed that dress wouldn't allow any underwear. And no tan lines. She likes sunbathing commando. That's hot!

My cock thickens immediately at the sight of the hard globes of her ass cheeks, my feet automatically walking toward them, my hands positioned and ready to grope them.

She moans and pushes her ass back when I cup each cheek, squeezing them. JJ quickly lowers the top of her dress and grabs her breasts.

I have a suspicion that no one has filled her in about the debauchery that goes on within the four walls of the Pleasure

Extraordinaire mansion and the intense competition we, the PE men, get into to satisfy our urges. We might have gone through a long and extensive training on women's sexual pleasure, but we all know their true pleasure comes from the satisfaction of our own selfish desires.

Words lose meaning when we're thrown in with fresh flesh; our minds shut off instantly. The beast mode is on. We rely on our senses. The smell of arousal. The pitch of moans. The heightened body heat. Droplets of perspiration. Back arching. Nipples peaking. Thighs squeezing against each other. Pussy swelling.

No talking for us. No thinking. Just acting and fucking. And it all comes automatically.

Her dress hits the floor, and she's stark-naked before us, save for her black high-heels. She might have initially thought she had some say in our play, but right now the only thing she has control over is her own breathing, and even that comes to a sudden halt every now and then when I or JJ hit an especially sweet spot.

I splay my hand on her back and push her down; exactly at the same time JJ unbuttons his jeans and releases his erection and forces it into her mouth. His fingers thread through her hair, his hand covering her head like a hat. She couldn't get away even if she wanted, not that there's a woman in existence who'd willingly abandon the wild peaks of pleasure that are about to come.

I hear her gagging, but soon, her head bobs up and down rhythmically against JJ's crotch.

I run my hand down the crack of her ass and pause at her clit. I can practically feel it throb against the pad of my thumb. One gentle rub followed by another, and her legs are already wobbly.

I stop, cutting out her pleasure, and listen to her wordless complaint through her moans, smiling to myself in satisfaction. The evidence of her arousal is leaking and soaking my fingers. I move my thumb between the lips of her pussy, and she lifts her ass higher in the air, opening up her love channel, like it wants to catch my finger.

She moans, aching, desire palpable in her

voice. My cock twitches, its desire to invade and conquer too big to control. I slip a finger into her opening to probe her pussy and test the waters before dipping my cock, literally in her case as the waters are streaming generously down her pussy.

A visible shiver runs through her body from inside out as I inch my finger deeper, rubbing around to find her weak spot. Her body reveals to me the answer by stilling when I hit a tight knot in the depths of her hungry pussy.

Smiling, I start massaging it, gently at first and then harder when her legs begin shaking. She rides my finger while expertly sucking JJ's cock. I continue stroking her through her convulsions and whimpers, without giving her a break. One orgasm ends while another starts, and those just with my fingers.

At some point, when I lose count of her orgasms, I finally give in to my cock's desire and release it. Its head finds her pussy without any direction from my hand. Smart, huh!

I hold the shaft nonetheless and thrust

into her. She squeaks in surprise. My cock is exploring the depths of her pussy, with her juices as my only shield—now that's much better than using a condom.

Baring my cock in front of Ace or any other man has never been a reason for concern for me, but Ace looks troubled and can't keep his eyes on the wild action taking place right before his face. Why in God's name did he open a brothel if he can't watch a good-quality live porn?

I pump and ride her as she struggles to keep the rhythm of her blowjob. My eyelids feel heavy, my body fully attuned to hers. I nearly miss the door opening.

JJ's body covers whoever it is that's standing in the doorway, but I can tell it's an unwelcome guest because Ace shoots up to his feet in a heartbeat and dashes around his desk.

"Lindsay!" he yells.

Cocking my head to the side, I glance at the silhouette behind JJ just to confirm my suspicion. Oh, well. Ace had his reason to look uncomfortable with our play, and that reason has a name. Lindsay frigging Doheny.

"What is going on here?" Her face contorted with horror and shock; Lindsay stares at Ace without blinking or moving.

Ace mirrors her, looking equally shocked, but there's also something else beneath that expression. And that's the look of shame for hurting someone who cares.

Ace is probably the last man on earth I should be jealous of, but right now I'd kill to have that look of embarrassment. I'd kill to have someone caring for me enough to get mad at me. I've been so occupied with my plans of overthrowing Michael that I've been able to overlook the excruciating pain in my chest.

The pain of loneliness and solicitude.

I couldn't even take a moment to grieve after my mother's death, Michael got me so worked up. But now, he's gone. He can't abuse me or my sister anymore. Now I can live and feel.

But, rather than happiness and freedom, all I feel is isolation.

Lindsay's eyes find me, shocked and terrified by the sight, stopping the world around me with one direct stare, and suddenly all I can see is myself through the lens of her eyes.

The sight is horrible to say the least. Me giving it to a total stranger while she's gulping another man's dick in the middle of an office. No emotions or words of endearment involved. No loving caresses. No kissing.

Why did I think there's pleasure in this messed-up, fake performance? How can I get any satisfaction out of such a degrading act that doesn't even involve a simple kiss? What person, man or woman, in their right mind would give a shit about me when I keep acting like an untamed animal?

Wincing at me, Lindsay lets out a shrill cry and spins on her heels, disappearing as quickly as she appeared.

Not wanting to continue this charade, I slide out of McKenzie and stride out of Ace's office, feeling dirty and belittled for the first time after many months of service at Pleasure Extraordinaire, and all it took was an unexpected confrontation by Lindsay.

CH 4 - The Wrong Boobs

"I want the church girl." I stand at the doorway of Julie's condo at ten at night.

She must have been dozing off or something because her eyes are hooded and about to close. A soft, "Excuse me," rolls off her lips along with a wide yawn. Her t-shirt and pajama bottoms aren't black, but green. Surprising! And when I peek through the open door, I note, with another surprise, she's not drowning in a complete black and gloomy life.

"You told me you'd find me a good, loyal girl who goes to church. I want her now." The five shots of tequila I gulped down before coming here has me slurring the r's, but I suppose she understands my words...or not?

"What are you talking about?" She yawns again and stretches her arms. For the first time in years, her hair isn't in a bun, but in a low ponytail—an improvement if you ask me. Who enjoys the sight of a giant second head? Well, not me.

"Can I come in?" Without waiting, I invite myself in. It's not like she'll have a man over, who'd be annoyed by my surprise visit. Even if she does, I'm her boss. My needs should have priority over a random man from a bar.

"Please!" she murmurs behind me in a mocking tone. "I bet you'd help yourself to liquor, but I don't have any alcohol at home. Feel free to drink as much coffee as you want, though."

"Yeah, I'd like that." I settle on the large cream sofa, spreading my arms around the back of it and stretching my legs out on the coffee table.

Her eyes narrow at me in fury, but she doesn't express her dismay. Her condo has an open floor design with a small kitchen area. Walking around the breakfast island barefoot, she pours water into the coffee machine and turns it on.

I smile when I notice her red-polished toenails. Nice! I'll add my observation on the short list of everything feminine about Julie. So far, I think I have two items on it.

"What was it about the church girl again?" she yells over the kitchen island as she fills the machine with coffee grounds.

"I want to marry," I intend to say, but again with the r's missing, I'm not sure what she's made of my words.

She chuckles and gives her head a brief shake, glancing at me as she walks back into the living room. "Did you have dinner?"

"No."

"Are you hungry?"

"No."

"You need to eat if you don't want to ruin your tomorrow with a hangover."

"I'll take an Advil."

"Advil won't help. I had lasagna from the dinner. Do you want some?"

I nod and watch her go back to the kitchen. Opening the fridge, she takes out a glass container with lasagna in it and a plate from the cupboard. She turns her back to me when she fills the plate with food. I lean my head against the back of the sofa and briefly close my eyes while listening to the soft noises she makes as she moves around the kitchen.

The house I live in has a living room bigger than her entire condo and several bedrooms that no one except for the housemaids enter. Julie's condo is the perfect size for a single person, not like the monster of a mansion I have and barely live in.

"How many bedrooms does your condo have?" I ask, my eyes still closed, my body ready to pass out.

"Two and a walk-in closet."

My eyes flutter open as I hear her footsteps on the hardwood floor of the living room. "Cozy place. Lovely location."

"Thanks." She sets the plate with lasagna and salad on the coffee table. "Now eat."

"That's a lot. I'll have to hit the gym early in the morning."

"That's better than hitting the bathroom to throw up."

I raise my hand and point at her with my index finger. "That's right." Grabbing the plate and the fork, I fill my stomach, barely noticing the taste of the food. "Thanks," I say when I place the empty plate back on the table. "It was delicious." At least it didn't sit heavily in my stomach. She might have a good point with the cooking abilities of the woman who'll mother my kids. "So, where's your list," I ask, words coming out of my mouth a little more clearly.

She grins and disappears down the hallway and comes back with a tablet. "This isn't the final list. Feel free to add or subtract anyone you want. Also, I'd appreciate it if you'd fill me in on the type of woman you have in mind."

I clasp my hands on my lap and stare ahead while thinking about the qualities of the woman who'll chain me down into monogamy. "She should look great, at least a nine on the scale of attractiveness."

Julie rolls her eyes in her typical 'here we go again' way. "Oh, please."

"Hear me out. It's no secret that I look great. I have money—tons of it. I'm wildly famous. I know what I'm bringing to the table. If I date a girl with less-than-delicious looks, I'll always think I can have done better. Besides, girls' looks deteriorate with time. If she starts with a solid nine, I won't mind if she turns into a seven or six over the years."

"You're disgusting."

"So I love big boobs and a firm ass. Sue me."

"Looks shouldn't matter when you find the one."

I let out a sigh of disappointment. She's been working for me and with me for longer than I can remember, but still fails to recognize my most basic needs. "Well, then why don't I marry my housemaid, Consuela? She's an excellent cook, far better than any five-star restaurant chef I know. She's diligent with her work all around the house, goes to church regularly, and even prays for my health and wellbeing. She's single and my age. I could turn her into a great housewife and mother of my kids, but I don't. Do you know why? This'll sound harsh, but it's because she weighs more than I do with her 5"0' height. All other qualities being equal, I'll pick a Victoria's Secret model who hasn't turned on an oven in her life over an excellent cook with mediocre looks."

"Ahh, you're a superfici—"

I raise my hand to stop her before she can assault me. "Don't call me that. I'm a man. I'm programmed to choose the prettier chick by nature, just like women pick wealthier guys as their mates. I'm wealthy. I can provide. So why shouldn't I have my pick of women?"

"You're absolutely right! I won't argue your tastes. After all, tastes are personal."

"That's my girl!" I cheer along with an appreciative smile. I love it when she agrees. In fact, it's sexy when she bows to my requests. Speaking of sexy, I feel a stir beneath my pants as blood starts pooling between my legs.

"You're rich," she continues mumbling as if she's talking to herself. "Your looks are off the charts. You've got everything a girl can dream of. Why shouldn't you choose the best possible woman as your mate?"

Pulling both her legs over the chair yoga style, she sits upright, straightening her shoulders. Her boobs stand up, and naturally my eyes fall to her chest. I can see the black bra through her cotton t-shirt and can even spot her poking nipples.

I know she's noticed my obvious ogling of her boobs because her arms abruptly cross over her chest as she nonchalantly keeps on her self-talk. "The girl of your dreams must exist, and I promise I'll find her for you."

I blink and quickly get up, heading for the door, my hand scratching the back of my head. "I trust you will. I gotta go now."

"Wait." She pushes to her feet as well and walks toward me, her arms still over her chest.

I hate to be the one to make her uncomfortable. She was sexually harassed for several years by my father, forced to service the sexual desires of his clients and business partners. Objectifying her body is the last thing I should do as her friend and her boss who's more than happy having her onboard. "Don't you want to know how the interviews for the writer position went?"

"We'll talk tomorrow." I push down the door handle and hurry out.

"Zane!" she calls out when I stand before the elevator. I turn toward her, still feeling guilty for staring at her boobs. "Are you free Friday night?"

I frown and consider my answer. "Yeah, I guess."

She leans against the doorframe, her arms falling to her sides, her cheeks flushing a little. "I'll set up your first date for seven p.m. Is that okay?"

"Sure." I'm a jerk for letting my gaze drop to her chest again, but, fortunately, the elevator door dings and I hop in.

"I'll call you with the details." I hear her yell before the doors close. What the hell is wrong with me? She's going to therapy to be able to heal from all the abuse she suffered, for Christ's sake. And she's my friend...in fact, my only true friend. How could I become one of those men who looks at her like she's a piece of meat?

I'm disgusting, and to avoid the feeling of disgust, I need to distract myself. My only options are alcohol or more pussy. I should probably stay away from both to honor my new promise to change and become a better man. But, I'm only human, and I can't strike both out of my life so soon.

So, I tell Daney to drive me to the apartment I bought for Penelope, the one and only lover I kept for longer than a year.

CH 5 - The Old Flame

I met Penelope the first day I started working at Hawkins Media Group, the day after my graduation, per Michael's order. She was there for an audition for a side role in a popular sitcom.

She was shy, but perky, a strange mixture that instantly grabbed my attention, and when I found out she was a virgin, I couldn't keep my hands away. She gave in to my advances pretty quickly and became my regular bedmate.

She didn't get the role, but I arranged for her to get a better one in another series and bought her a condo. Over the years, she became obsessed with me, though she never questioned my promiscuity. I kept going back to her after every argument I had with Michael, and she'd calm my nerves with utmost care.

Soon, she started appearing as my date at galas and special events. The media attention brought her offers to appear in several blockbuster movies. She could have hit it big. Very big. She had the chance and the talent, but failed to take advantage of it.

Why? Because of her obsession with me. She made me a priority in her life. She'd rather attend to my sexual needs than learn her lines. She'd show up at movie sets without having a clue about the script because I kept her awake the entire night and she wouldn't utter a single word about my selfishness.

After one failure after another, producers put her on the stay-the-hell-away-from list. She didn't have a life outside of me interesting enough even to get a reality show. She'd become the pathetic mistress, who couldn't even get knocked up by her lover to save her life.

I kept her as my lover mostly out of pity, but also because she was eager and always available, like the perfect mistress. Until one day at a party Michael organized to make his fake relationship with Lindsay public. That day, Penelope left me coldheartedly, without even saying a word.

She changed the locks of the condo I bought for her and blocked my phone number and email address.

I haven't seen her in months and miss her gentle care to push away the dark clouds in my head. The feeling of disgust and loneliness that's weighing me down right now is too much to bear. Either I'll sink myself into her or drawn in alcohol.

I knock on the door of her condo. Once, twice, three times. I know when she peeks through the peephole because I've heard her footsteps.

"Penelope, open the door," I say softly, my face close to the door.

"Go away!" she yells, but hesitation is thick in her voice.

I haven't seen her in months; I have no idea if she has another man in her life.

"I need you," I whisper.

Seconds pass. Minutes. She's still on the

other side of the door, listening. I can feel her defenses breaking, can hear the protests in her mind drowning out. The longer I wait at her doorway, the weaker she'll become.

"Please, Penelope. I need you."

The door opens and she stands before me, her blonde hair around her shoulders, her body still in perfect shape, her eyes wet with tears. A tank top generously displays the tops of her braless breasts, and short shorts around her slim hips expose her long, tanned legs. She's mouthwatering.

I yank the door closed and launch myself over her, pushing her against the wall. She wilts beneath my body and lifts her teary eyes to mine, her green irises begging me to leave.

Holding the back of her head, I crush my lips against hers and dig my tongue into her mouth. A soft moan mixed with a sob is her reaction and it makes her even more desirable. My other hand travels down her throat and slides beneath her tank top, cupping her breast. She pushes her chest against my grip, her nipple hardening against my skin.

"Don't do it to me again," she pleads,

breathless in between our wet kisses.

Ignoring her pleas, I reach for the waistband of her shorts and pull them down, lowering my hand to her bare pussy, touching the soft, hairless skin, probing the tender flesh. She's wet and eager despite her weak protests, and bucks her hips against my hands.

"Let me in," I whisper to her. "I need you." I stroke her clit and capture her bottom lip with my teeth, gently pulling it.

"No," she squeals, pushing her hands against my chest. Her eyes sad, her expression confused, her lips swollen from my kisses, her breasts exposed, she moves away from me. However, my finger remains between the lips of her pussy, the pad of my thumb rubbing tenderly against her labia.

She turns her head to her side and closes her eyes, looking ashamed of her reaction against my hand. Her clit quivers with want, her lips whispering quiet protests one after another.

Her weakness is my strength, the reason why I've kept coming back to her.

"I want you!" I urge and flip her around,

her back against me, and pull her ass against my crotch, grinding myself against her soft ass cheeks until I'm rock hard.

Releasing my cock through the fly of my pants, I press the head against her wet opening and wait for her to take over. I know I'm playing with her mind for leaving that decision to her but I wait for her to wiggle her ass and open up for me.

And open up she does, sliding her swollen pussy lips around my cock, her inner walls convulsing hard as they swallow my shaft in a hungry gulp. I pull back before filling her completely, but she grinds and pushes against me.

I can hear her sobs getting louder with each thrust of my cock. I hate hearing her cry, being the reason for her tears. I've heard enough sobs in my life that I can't bear the sound of it anymore. It hurts my ears and slashes my soul.

On the other hand, her tears are the proof that her heart is still beating for me. Why should I go through the trouble of seeking a woman good enough to share my life with, when there's already a girl who meets all the criteria, plus loves me deeply for who I am?

She's familiar with my darkness and knows the scars of my soul that'll never recover no matter how many therapy sessions I attend. Not just that, she's become expert at distracting me and making me forget about my pain, albeit momentarily. I should give her a chance. She's stood by me for so many years; that's the only fair thing to do.

With renewed keenness, I circle my hands around her slim waist to thrust harder into her, allowing the rhythmic slaps of our bodies as the only distraction to my senses. Her sobs turn into moans of ecstasy quickly, and her hands reach back and grab my hips to encourage me to ram harder into her. I do and give her the rough strokes that she needs to come.

Closing my eyes, I throw my head back, pushing away all thoughts and embracing the softness of her body enmeshed around me. Her pussy starts pulsating; her body tenses in an instant, and a loud shrill cry escapes her lips when she reaches her peak. Then, she stills. Her body goes limp, as she collapses into my arms when the waves of orgasm subside. Her vitality is gone and transferred into me.

She's given me a piece of herself and trusted me with her vulnerability.

That's the difference between fucking a long-term lover and a random woman, and as much as I love variety, sex in an established relationship is more satisfying.

My cock becomes harder inside her surrendered body, my balls tight and aching. Wrapping my arms around her, I slide into her harder and jet my release inside her, inhaling her familiar perfume, burying my face in her hair.

I hold her tight for long moments until I'm flaccid and my cock slides out of her. She turns around to face me and rests her head against my chest, her sobs back in full force. My chest tightens as the sound of her sobs echo in my ears.

Holding her chin, I urge her to face me. "Why are you crying?"

She glances up at me with sad eyes. Those aren't the tears of joy after reaching an earth-shattering orgasm. She's crying because she's miserable.

She'd never had a happy and optimistic constitution and her gloomy mood has soured even more over the years, perhaps due to my lack of commitment. I hate being the reason for her heartache, but her dark mood reminds me of the very reason why I never considered being exclusive with her.

She doesn't have Lindsay's strength and unbreakable willingness to survive and be happy on her own. I have enough black clouds in my life; I can't handle carrying someone else's misery, too.

I need someone to lift me up and show me the sunny side of life, not to weigh me down with depression. If I choose Penelope to be my only mate, we'll drown each other with our sorrow, and it's no good for either of us.

"I love you, Zane. I'll always love you." She runs her fingers along my jaw, her eyes locked on mine. "But this was a mistake. We both know it. I can't allow you back into my life. I'm still in the process of getting over you."

Her words make me feel relieved and

angry in equal parts. I'm not used to being turned down.

"I'm aware you'll never love me back the way I love you. I wish you did, but I can't hang onto that hope anymore," she continues. "I met someone else. He's caring and ready to commit to me."

Another man? I should have thought of that. "Who is he?" I frown and pull my hands back from her body, my anger tensing my muscles.

She trembles without the support of my hands, her eyes growing large in shock and dismay. "It doesn't matter. I'm only trying to say that this won't happen again. You're not capable of giving me what I need, so you have to respect my decision to move on."

"You don't know what kind of men there are out there. They'll use you and take advantage of you until you become useless to them." I've been in her life for long enough to know she's not the brightest bulb out there and prioritizes the wrong qualities in men.

"You should know," she says with a sarcastic tone. "You've been one such man. You used me for years and fucked me along with hundreds of other women. I don't think any other man will stoop lower than that."

Ouch! But, she's right. "I just want the best for you."

"The best for me?" Her lips curve into a painful smile. "If you wanted the best for me, you wouldn't have wasted my best years. You gave me nothing but eight miserable years. Have you any idea how much it hurts to see you going to another woman, reading news about you being involved with someone else? I can't continue living like this. I'm done. I need someone who'll cherish me and only me."

"Penelope, I'm sorry for what I did to you. I'm ready to—" A knock on the front door interrupts me.

"Penelope!" A man yells from behind the door.

"Oh, God!" Penelope quickly pulls up her shorts and straightens her tank top, wiping the tears away as she heads for the door. I tug my flaccid cock back in and zip up, curious about the unexpected visitor.

Coughing to clear my throat, I stand tall behind Penelope while she opens the door.

"Emmett," she says and throws herself into the visitor's arms.

Emmett Nielson. The son of the owner of Nielson industries and Nielson Network Channel, which means one of HMG's main competitors. Is Emmett now Penelope's new lover? I doubt he'll be able to fill up the emptiness I left in her heart and...well also in her pussy. I can't even imagine him even trying to give her half the pleasures I've given her over the years. It's laughable, really. Not because he's in his forties with his weak body and receding hairline, but also he's a pussy. He's never grown out of his father's shadow and even once pushed the company into bankruptcy during the one time his father trusted the company to him. Penelope is selling herself short.

"Penelope." He shoots me a sharp glare, his voice demanding. "What is he doing here?" He steps in the condo with an unshakable confidence as if he owns the entire building and grabs Penelope's hand possessively.

"He just, ahh." Penelope's voice trembles along with her lips while she's trying to come up with an excuse for my unexpected visit.

"Hello, Emmett." I cut her off to save her from the awkward situation. "The real question is; what are you doing in the condo I bought for my lover?"

He attempts to laugh at my comment, but it comes out pathetic and weak, just like everything else about him. "She's not your lover and she doesn't need you anymore." Then, he turns to Penelope, softening his voice. "Isn't that so, Penelope?"

"Yes. I'll move out." She covers their entwined hands with her other hand and moves closer into his body.

"You don't have to. It might be a gift from me, but it's yours. Keep it or sell it. It's up to you," I say curtly.

Penelope's eyes drift back and forth between Emmett and me, hesitation and worry clear in her glance.

As much as I despise Emmett, it's not my place to pick the right lover for Penelope, and I'd be an asshole if I came between her new lover and her. "I'll go now. Call me if you need anything." I walk past Emmett and stop at the doorway to give him one last glance of warning.

"You're walking a thin line," he calls after me, his tone intimidating. "I'd be very careful if I were you."

Two heavily built men in black suits wait in front of the door, along with another one in front of the elevator, and all look ready to attack. I consider my chances were Emmett to sic his men on me. Basically, null. But, he's not that much of a fool to have me beat up in a relatively public place with surveillance cameras and potential witnesses all around. If he wants to strike, which I have a strong belief that he will, he'll do it with much less risk of getting caught.

"Did he fuck you?" I hear him ask Penelope as I leisurely walk toward the elevator. Penelope's answer "No," comes out almost inaudible and I wonder how she'll explain my sperm leaking out of her pussy. I don't hear the rest of their conversation after the door closes with a loud bang. I consider going back in case Emmett gets violent and hurts Penelope physically, but decide against it and instead ask the doorman of the building to check up on Penelope in half an hour.

Penelope is out of my life for good. There's no way in hell I'll take her back after knowing the kind of man she allows into her life. I have neither the will nor the appetite to go back to Pleasure Extraordinaire to bang women just to have a release, either. I still have a list of lovers I can find comfort from, but they won't be any better than Penelope in terms of quality. Which leaves me no option but to seriously consider giving Julie's plan a chance.

Risk has always been a big part of my life, my existence, and my success. The only risk I'll be running with Julie's plan is wasting time. The investment of a little time is worth the risk if there's a chance I'll find a woman who'll chase away my sorrow and make me commit to her.

CH 6 - The Distraction

"When I said 'find me a church girl,' I didn't necessarily mean she should sing in the church choir." Standing in Julie's office, I scan the paper she has just stuffed into my hand.

Felicia Burton is twenty-eight, a devout Catholic, a nurse at the pediatrics unit at LA Community Hospital, born and raised in San Diego, and has had only one boyfriend with whom she broke up after he joined the military.

Julie shrugs and shifts her eyes back to the screen of her computer. "So what? She believes in God and prays for the good of the world every Sunday!"

"What am I going to talk to her about?

How many deadly sins I commit on a daily basis?"

Her eyes locked on her computer screen, she grins, making me wonder if the amusing look on her face is the result of my joke or something she's reading on the screen. "Just give her a chance. If it doesn't work out, we'll adjust the parameters, okay?"

"Whatever." I head for the door, impatient to get out of the office to have lunch.

"Brad asked for an urgent meeting. I told him you'd stop by the set during your lunch break." She brings her eyes up to my face and winces as if she's been caught making a mistake. "It's about the writers' team."

"Didn't you already fill the post?"

"I picked someone, but Brad thinks he's not suitable."

My eyebrow raises in curiosity, and I step back and turn to her fully, feeling my hunger abandon me. "Why not?"

"I don't know. I guess that's what he wants to discuss with you."

"Okay. I'll go see him."

"Would you mind if I tag along?" she

requests sweetly. "I'm curious about what he has to say."

"You could have asked him directly."

"I did, but he wants to speak only with you."

"Okay." I shrug. "You can come."

She nods and quickly gathers her tablet and purse. "I heard from Scarlett that he invited Henrietta Cruz over to his office twice this past week. I think he's considering her for the post."

"Henrietta Cruz, from Nielson Network Channel?" I laugh at Julie's suggestion. Brad is smart enough not to invite a spy into our team.

"Sounds silly, I know, but he might be onto something. He's been postponing my attempts to meet with him to talk about the candidate I picked for the post." She hurries to catch up with my steps as we walk down the hall to the elevators. "I'm not completely against having Henrietta on our team. She's talented, but in generic sitcoms, not necessarily in drama."

"Not to mention the fact that she'll be transferring from Nielson's," I add and get into the elevator, pushing the button for the garage after Julie steps in beside me.

"Yeah, but what can she do? It's not like Nielson's will try to get insider info on the script and copy Frat House. It's a recipe for failure."

"Still. Anything to do with Nielson's is a red flag for me. For all we know, she can intentionally sabotage the success of the show."

We hurry toward my car, and I open the door for Julie. She gets inside quickly and hands me her tablet once I slide in next to her in the backseat. As Daney drives out of the building, I read the resume of the candidate Julie picked for the screenwriter post.

"I know he doesn't look like a strong candidate just from his resume," Julie says, interrupting my reading. "But he has brilliant ideas about the directions the show can take. He pointed out the weaknesses the show had during the last two episodes, and I think they were all right on. I firmly believe we should add him to the team, if not for anything but to bring in fresh ideas."

Her enthusiasm while defending the

candidate speaks volumes about him, but also makes me curious why Brad is less than impressed. Julie asks me to scroll down the resume to find the ideas the candidate suggested for the upcoming episodes. I go through the bullet points one by one, commenting on the ones I like, throughout the ride.

Coincidently, Scarlet pulls up in the gated garage just at the same time Daney stops the car engine. She hurries out of the car and waits before the passenger door for us to get out.

The red summer dress she's wearing accentuates her youthfulness and liveliness, and, of course, her long legs. With her high-heels, she stands close to my height, a minor detail that has me fantasizing about pounding into her ass while standing up. Very briefly, though, before I remind myself of her irreplaceable role in Frat House. I can't afford to lose her, that's why I should erase any naughty thoughts about her this instant.

"Julie, great to see you again," Scarlet chirps and gives Julie a side hug. I frown and motion with my head to inquire without words about their unusual display of friendship, mostly because Julie has never been touchy-feely with anyone, much less with her colleagues.

"Hey, there, girl. How have you been?" Julie asks, ignoring my questioning glances and walks with Scarlet toward the entrance.

"Busy as always. My mom, grandma, and seven brothers are coming over tomorrow for my birthday, and I came in to go over the script with Troy."

Amused, I listen to their conversation about Scarlet's birthday plans as I follow them into the building and then to the elevator. Kindly enough, she invites me and Julie to the small party she's planning to organize at her home. Julie accepts her invitation for both of us and adds the date on my calendar before the elevator doors open.

Melinda at reception informs Scarlet of Troy's meeting with his stylist. Disappointed, Scarlet asks if she can join us while waiting for Troy. Although the meeting with Brad is mainly administrative, I see no reason why she shouldn't be part of the decision-making process. I nod with a wink and open the door to Brad's office.

Brad tries his best to hide his discomfort over me showing up with Julie and Scarlet beneath a forced smile and welcomes us into his office. Without wasting time with small talk, he directly starts raving about Henrietta and what an incredible addition she'll be for the writers' team.

I listen to him intently, even though I'm not thrilled about having someone from Emmett's company in mine. But it's not the first time someone has changed boats in this business. Sometimes enemies can make the best friends, and Henrietta could possibly change the direction of Frat House's future for the better. She certainly has the necessary experience.

"I'm not sure if she'll be a good fit for the team," I say, not to dismiss Julie's candidate right away.

"Henrietta is an award-winner writer, not some wannabe writer from rural Pennsylvania," Brad insists. "If anything, we'll be lucky to get her."

"Carry isn't a wannabe writer," Julie defends her favorite candidate. "He might not have awards lined up like Henrietta, but it doesn't change the fact that he's creative and obsessed with Frat House. He knows all the episodes down to each line. Can you say that about Henrietta? I doubt if she knows the full title of the show."

"It doesn't matter how much she knows about it. She can learn," Brad says calmly, although the redness on his face speaks of nothing but the simmering anger brewing inside him.

I glance over at Scarlet, who seems to be uncomfortable with the direction the conversation is headed. As our eyes meet, she straightens up in her chair and gives me a shy grin. "I know it's not my business," she says, holding my gaze. "I'm just an actress, after all, but I—"

Brad immediately cuts her off with a loud and harsh tone. "Scarlet, please stay out of it!"

Scarlet's jaw drops in shock, and she nods, looking utterly embarrassed. "I'm very sorry."

"No." I lift my hand to stop Brad from talking. "Go ahead, Scarlet. Say what you wanted to say. We value everyone's opinion."

"It's just my personal opinion, but I used to be a big fan of Troubled Girls back when it was a big hit. Do you remember how it went downhill in the middle of the third season? I heard Henrietta became the head of the writers of the show around that time."

"It's just a coincidence. The show was bound to die since they decided to kill off one of the main characters," Brad says, now unable to hide the fury in his voice.

"No, Scarlet is right," Julie says. "It was actually Henrietta's idea to kill off that character. Ask anyone you want, everyone knows she was the reason for the change in the scripts."

Brad shakes his head and draws in a long breath of air. "Still, it's too risky to hire a no-name writer. Henrietta is our best bet. She's full of great and fresh ideas for the next episodes."

I know a fruitless discussion when I hear it, and this is becoming one, especially because I feel a headache coming. "Rather than discussing it to death, why don't we ask them both to come up with a general outline for the next few episodes?" I start to stand, not wanting to be in this office, much less continue the discussion.

"I think that's a great idea." Julie gets to her feet quickly.

"Wait, really?" Brad softens his voice when speaking. "I'm not sure asking Henrietta to write up the next episodes without paying her anything is a good idea."

"Well, if she isn't already brewing up some ideas, she's not good for us anyway." I shrug and move to the door.

Scarlet hooks the strap of her bag over her shoulder and follows me and Julie out. "I should have kept my mouth shut," she whispers to Julie apologetically, but Julie gives her head a quick shake to encourage her participation.

"Don't apologize for wanting the best for the show." I glance down at her sideways and see her cheeks flush at my words. She looks adorable, more so because she's chewing her bottom lip mindlessly.

Here's a stellar example of a strong, beautiful, and industrious girl who has a goal to achieve and lets nothing else distract her along the way. She knows her place, but doesn't shy away from pointing out the truth. And, let's not forget about the small but significant fact that she's not fazed by the numerous men chasing after her. If only she didn't work for me...

My headache intensifies despite leaving Brad's office. "Clear my schedule for the rest of the day. I'll work from home," I say to Julie.

"How about your date with Felicia? Shall I postpone it to tomorrow night?" Julie produces her phone quickly and opens up my calendar, looking ready to type in whatever I order.

"Oh, you have a date?" Scarlet chimes in, staring at me with curious eyes. "Do I know her?"

"No, no one knows her," Julie answers for me. "She's a nurse and not a famous one as far as I know. That's kind of the point, though. Zane doesn't need someone from the entertainment industry."

"Really?" Scarlet says with a hint of disappointment in her voice. It's adorable to say the least and has me running my eyes over her tight body. Has she considered herself as a suitable partner for me? From her deepening blush, I'd say yes, which should be my clue to end my obvious ogling.

Luckily, Julie comes to my rescue and explains to her the reasons why it's a better idea for me to get involved with a low-key woman with a modest lifestyle, rather than a camera-crazed woman who worships nothing but diamonds and Botox. Scarlet doesn't look satisfied with Julie's explanation, and I don't blame her.

As we approach the front door of the building, Julie stops to give Scarlet a friendly hug. And to my utter astonishment, after their hug Scarlet moves from Julie and approaches me with open arms, clearly wanting to give me a hug, too. I should be a better man and just move away. Even though I'd look like a socially awkward asshole, it's still better than the alternative scenario where I give her any kind of hope. But I don't. I spread my arms open for her and wrap them tightly around her tiny waist. Not just that, I lift her up a little, and she gives me a surprised squeal.

Julie grabs me by the elbow and hauls me out. As soon as we're out of Scarlet's hearing range, Julie starts her lecture. "That was totally unprofessional, in case you haven't noticed. She's only twenty-two and very likely a virgin. She idolizes you. Don't screw with her mind. It won't do any good for anyone."

"I just couldn't help myself."

"Even your excuse is repulsive. Get yourself together. Save your dirty thoughts for the woman who'll be your wife."

"I find myself wishing it was Scarlet."

"You're not serious."

"I'm not. She's just too sexy for me to ignore. That's all there is to it." And very sweet, but I'll keep that to myself. "I'll stay away from her. I love Hawkins Media Group way too much to ruin its most successful show."

CH 7 - The Church Girl

"I'll have mushroom gnocchi and Greek salad, please." Felicia hands the waiter the menu and reaches for her glass of ginger ale. Yep, she doesn't drink alcohol, doesn't even know the taste since she has never even felt inclined to try an alcoholic drink.

"I'll have the same." I smile at her when she glances at me with a surprised look.

"Now I feel guilty for not ordering the roast duck."

"Don't. I'm vegetarian."

"Really?" Her eyes travel down my chest as if she'll find a confirmation there for or against my declaration. "I never pegged you for a vegetarian."

"And you won't be the first one. It's okay, though. I've never felt comfortable eating meat. How about you?"

"I love chicken, but that's about it." She grins and sets her glass of ginger ale beside her empty plate. "Um. I'm surprised you replied to my message. I mean, you and I are from different worlds. You must be surrounded by beautiful women, whereas I'm an average girl with an average job."

Surrounded doesn't even begin to cover it. Drowning in, or suffocated by, fits the bill better. But, with her full chest, lean waistline, and long brown hair, she's far from being an average girl. Add her large chocolate-brown eyes and luscious lips to the mix, she's easily an eight. And all that without makeup. She definitely fulfills the requirements in the looks department.

I shake my head playfully and lean closer to the table to whisper to her the truth, "I see what I see, and there's nothing average about it. You're beautiful, absolutely gorgeous."

She grins, slightly pushing her shoulders forward, and lowering her eyes to the table in slight embarrassment. "Thank you."

Finally, a woman who accepts a compliment without feeling guilty...makes me want to praise her even more. "So, what made you decide to become a nurse?"

She licks her bottom lip and slowly lifts her gaze at me, hesitating to look me in the eye. So different than the women I'm familiar with, the kind who would shamelessly seduce every eligible man. "I just loved the idea of saving lives. My parents didn't have the money for med school for me to become a doctor, and I certainly didn't have the patience. I couldn't be happier with my job. I love taking care of sick children and assuring their parents that their kids are well taken care of. There's no better feeling in the world for me than the feeling of caring for children."

"That's admirable." Is it naughty of me to imagine her in a slutty nurse costume? It won't be a costume in her case, though, since she's a real nurse. "Do you have any hobbies?"

"Not really. I mean, I help out at the food shelter most of my down time. Also, I read for the blind members of my community at the local library. They're wonderful people, and I feel honored to have the chance to serve to them."

Have I mistakenly taken Mother Teresa out on a date? As gorgeous as this girl might be, her generosity is humbling and makes me want to get to know her better. "You're great. I wish I had the time to help out people in need." My wickedness probably comes through with my fake wish, but I'm not a hopeless case. Everyone, even I, has a good side inside them, and this girl might just be the right one to help me become my better self.

"You don't have to be present to help. Keeping the poor and disadvantaged people in your prayers will always do wonders."

Fortunately, our orders arrive before tears start to pool in my eyes for the magnitude of goodness Felicia has in her heart. We dive into the delicious food, while exchanging little tidbits about our lives and personalities. She talks about her one and only hobby, riding horses, and the entire time she talks about it, I find myself visualizing her riding me cowgirl style.

But, according to Julie, I'm not even allowed to kiss her on our first date, much less let her ride me. And, I don't think Felicia would be onboard with having any sexual contact before marriage anyway. I'll have to find a way to convince her to allow me a test drive before getting myself into a life-long commitment. All a matter of time, though. For now, I enjoy her beautiful smile and the occasional display of the top of her boobs along with a cheerful conversation.

She admires the leather seats of my limousine as Daney drives us to her home after the dinner. "This is a beautiful car. Do you have other cars?"

"Yeah, several. I'm afraid I don't know how many."

"Oh." She tilts her head to the side with a slightly disapproving look on her face. "It's okay. There's nothing wrong with indulging yourself in nice things, as long as you donate a good portion of your fortune to the less fortunate."

"Yeah, I donate a lot." To decrease my taxable income, but it's money given to the poor, nonetheless. Does it matter the motivation behind it? "I donated ten thousand dollars just last month for the ovarian cancer cause."

My words light up her eyes and she gives me a long look of marvel. "You're a wonderful man." Her words are like honey, and I can't help but smile in pride. She might just have found a way to turn me into a money-giving machine.

"Here we are, ma'am," Daney calls out from his seat and stops the car before a three-story apartment building on Fairfax Avenue.

"Thank you very much. I really appreciate it." Felicia smiles at Daney, although his back is turned to her, then she faces me. "Would you like to come up for a cup of coffee? I have a few booklets I'd like to share with you in case you're looking to widen your portfolio of charitable causes."

"I would be honored to hear your suggestions," I say, probably way too eagerly, but there's something about her that makes me want to donate half my inheritance to appease her. "Daney, would you mind waiting for me for a few minutes?"

"No, sir." Daney glances up at me from

the rearview, looking confused about my unusual kindness. I clear my throat and climb out of the car, while Daney hurries out to get Felicia's door.

Perhaps unaccustomed to having men opening doors for her, she eagerly thanks Daney and slips her arm through mine as we walk toward the building she lives in. It's an old, three-story building with probably six or seven units, and she lives on the first floor in a one-bedroom apartment.

I hand her my coat and stroll into the cozily decorated living room, which has flowers left and right, mostly orchids. As she disappears into the kitchen to get the coffee machine going, I settle on the blue loveseat and pick up the book lying on the coffee table.

The History of Religion, says the title. I skim through the table of contents while occasionally glancing at the tall bookcase across from me. It's filled with books, probably a hundred of them. The urge to call Julie to congratulate her for setting me up with a perfect blind date overwhelms me, and I almost pull my phone out of the pocket of my dress pants to send her a text, but Felicia shows up, carrying a tray with two cups of coffee.

I stand to take the tray out of her hands and lay it on the coffee table, beside the religion book. "Your library is impressive. You didn't tell me you loved reading."

"I love reading with a passion." She smiles, blushing as if she's confessed something embarrassing, although there's nothing wrong about a woman who reads. It shows how smart she is and that's sexy.

"This one looks interesting." I point out the religion book and lift a cup of coffee.

"It's a wonderful book with lots of insights about other religions. I'm a devout Catholic myself, but I find other religions fascinating as well. Did you know Hell doesn't exist according to Judaism, and Sufi believers are called *fuqara*, which means poor?"

I don't think I've ever heard of the word Sufi before. So, I just raise my eyebrows to show her how interesting I find the little facts she's shared with me.

She gives me yet another apologetic

glance. "I'm boring you, aren't I?" She purses her lips, peeking up at me through her thick, long lashes.

"Absolutely not!" I start to say, but she cuts me off by pressing her index finger against my lips. I wasn't expecting any physical contact, much less such an intimate move. She's definitely full of surprises and knows how to get under my skin.

We stare at each other for long moments, without either of us attempting to make a move, then she shifts on the couch to get closer to me and locks her eyes with mine, catching me off-guard when our faces are only an inch apart.

Her skin is flawless even from up-close and her scent wafts to me in sweet waves. Chewing her bottom lip, she pulls her finger from my lips down my jaw, her touch turning on my male instincts in an instant. All her sweet qualities fade away in the background of her shining beauty and silky skin, and an acute impulse to infiltrate her and make her mine takes over.

I should be a better man and fight against it. She doesn't know what she's causing with her close proximity. She's pure. I should respect her and not push matters.

She comes closer despite my best efforts and brushes her lips against mine, softly, sweetly, taking her time to taste every curve of my lips. Her eyes close, while I keep mine open to admire her charms, as we probe each other's lips. She tastes like the chocolate mousse we ate for dessert, making me want to devour the depths of her mouth.

Her hands push against my chest, and I make sure to flex my muscles beneath my shirt to give her a hint of my hard body. She moans softly into my mouth and pushes her body closer, molding it into mine.

This is a sweet make-out session, I keep telling my mind, that's ordering me to pin her down and have my way with her. Her pussy must be in desperate need of the special care my able mouth and fingers could provide, not to mention my hardening cock, but I shouldn't let my urges get the better of me. I should respect her limits. We're only testing our physical attraction and chemistry. I shouldn't read too much into it. She'll run for the hills if I try and show her my physical needs on our first date.

Her hands on my torso move south. My breathing becomes shorter, my cock thick and raging, despite my best efforts to keep my body in check. She's very likely not familiar with the male libido, much less mine. Otherwise, she'd know how quickly the touch of her hands can turn me into a sexual beast.

Or, maybe this is the religious girl's game. Seducing but not having sex until she's sure of her place in my life. I must say, it's working. I'll not be able to get her out of my mind tonight, or any of the following nights, until I bury my cock inside her. The idea of not being able to fuck her tonight turns me on and has my cock throbbing painfully.

Her hand lowers even more and she hooks her fingers around the waistband of my pants, her lips continuing their sweet massage on mine. But, to my astonishment, she reaches for the button of my pants, undoes it, and then unzips my pants.

What's she up to? If she so much as touches my cock, I won't be able to leave her alone. I'll need supernatural powers to be able to get out of her home without touching her.

Despite the slow strokes of her lips against mine, her hands are uncomfortably quick and slip beneath my boxers; and before I know it, she's palming my cock. Everything stops moving at that point, the entire evening turning upside down.

What she's doing with her hands tightly around my cock isn't seduction any more , it's sex, no matter how you look at it. As if that wasn't shocking enough, she pulls her mouth away from my face and quickly moves down to my crotch, closing her moist lips around my cock. Not that I'd ever decline a sexy woman wanting to go down on me, but her eagerness is a complete surprise. I'm getting a blowjob from practically a stranger without even having to ask for it.

She takes my cock deeper into her wet, hot mouth, sucking its head with enthusiasm, while I lean back against the back of the couch and throw my head back, my eyes closed, my limbs relaxed, my entire blood supply pooled between my legs. She's very talented at what she's doing and has me coming all over her mouth within minutes, and swallows every drop of it eagerly.

"That was amazing," I mutter, looking down at her through my hooded eyes. "The entire evening was great. Thank you."

Grinning in satisfaction, she wipes her swollen lips with the back of her hand. "You're welcome."

The easy way the words come out of her mouth makes me wonder how many other men have enjoyed her mouth. The thought instantly destroys all the attraction that's been growing in me for her. "This was lovely, but it's getting late. I have an early meeting tomorrow." I get to my feet and get my coat from the small closet by the door.

She races behind me and opens the door for me. "Are you going to call me?"

I hate the hesitation in her voice, but I can't help the instant turn-off in my head. "Sure!" The lie rolls out of my lips easily as I move to her face and leave a quick kiss on her cheek. "Take care."

"Good night." She waves after me.

CH 8 - The Reminder

I ask Daney to drive me to Julie's home, hoping to find her there so she can explain to me what the hell went wrong with the woman she picked for me. Julie frowns when she opens the door and finds out it's no other than me, her boss, bothering her late in the night.

"Sorry to disturb you at this hour. Can I come in?" I ask.

She rolls her eyes at me with a questioning look and adjusts the belt of her green robe as she lets me in. I come close to letting my eyes run down below her hips to see if she's wearing any pants beneath her robe but hurry inside to shake away such inappropriate thoughts. I don't have a single idea of what's wrong with me. The more women I fuck, the more I want, it seems. It's not completely wrong, after all it's a biological response, but I shouldn't allow any sexual thoughts about Julie to contaminate my mind and ruin a perfectly good friendship.

Oblivious to my momentary distraction, Julie curls up on an armchair and pulls the hem of her robe over her legs, covering everything 'til her ankles. Good girl!

I get myself comfortable on the large couch and fill her in on the details of my date including the part where Felicia eagerly swallowed my cock.

"So what if she blew you. She must have been thinking that's the standard treatment you get from women, and she didn't want to fall behind in the race," Julie defends Felicia.

"What race? All I could think of afterward was trying to calculate how many other men she must have sucked off."

"You, of all men, have to wonder that!" She rolls her eyes, rightly so, but that's what it is and I can't change my tastes.

"It's really disappointing. She was so

sweet at first. I was impressed by her kindness and generosity to the people in need."

"Well, she's generous for sure, for helping out with your load on your first date," Julie points out with a giggle.

Ignoring her comment, I continue my pouting. "The whole conversation about me getting married was about finding the right girl, and I'll risk sounding like an asshole, but a girl who has had a lot of men in her life makes me suspicious of her loyalty to me. I don't want to be cheated on a few years down the road. Does that make sense?"

She shakes her head. "The same logic applies to you. You've had, what, thousands of women in your life. So, that makes you prone to cheat, too, doesn't it?"

"No. Not necessarily. When I make a decision, I follow through with it. If I decide to commit to a girl, I won't stray. But I must be absolutely sure of her loyalty for that to happen. Any single doubt, even temporary, will ruin it for me."

She takes in a long breath of air, giving her head another disapproving shake. "I don't get it."

"That's okay. I must say I was impressed by her until the last minutes. I even thought she could easily win my heart and turn me into a happy puppy, but she blew it."

"What comes now?" she asks. "Do you still want to continue dating? I have 19 other candidates I thought you might like."

"Sure. The worst case scenario, I'll get my nuts rocked off by nineteen other women."

"You know you're talking to a girl, right?" She winces and gets to her feet, her arms tightly crossed across her chest.

"Yeah. Kind of. I'm very sorry. I'll cut the bullshit." I look around the living room, not wanting to leave soon. If I go back to my home, I'll probably find an excuse to drink. "Do you want to watch a movie together? We can order pizza, too."

Her face beams instantly, and she smiles. "I'd love that. I bought He's just not that into you last month and never got around to watching it."

I almost start rolling my eyes in boredom, but I restrain myself and nod sheepishly.

"Just kidding," she says and laughs. "I

have Ender's Game, Thor, and Pacific Rim. Which one do you want?"

"Wow, really? All sound good. You pick."

"Let's start with Thor. We can change to something else if it gets boring." She stands and, on her way to the DVD player, trips on a chair leg and falls on her butt. Her elbows hit the floor and she groans in pain.

"Shouldn't you have figured out this whole walking thing by now?" I joke as I run to help her up, but stop cold in my tracks, when I notice her silky white thighs exposed under her robe. Her skin looks soft and smooth, and my fingers twitch to run along the perfect smoothness.

Her crimson cheeks catch my attention, and I realize my indiscreet gazing. She quickly covers herself, pushes up to her feet, and casually walks to the DVD player to start the movie. All the while I gaze at her, paralyzed and speechless. Perhaps to escape the intense air in the room, she goes to the kitchen to order pizza and coke.

As my mind fights to erase the image of her bare legs, I find myself settling back into the couch. When the movie starts, she settles next to me on the couch, pulling a blanket over her.

"How come you never go out on dates?" I ask.

She frowns, looking insulted by my question. "I do go out on dates."

"I mean with someone other than yourself," I joke with a laugh, while she picks up a cushion and throws it at me. I catch it and tuck in beneath my arm, still curious about her answer. "When was the last time you let a man take you out?"

She fixes her eyes on the ceiling, thinking. "Um, I had lunch with Tony, from accounting last month, but nothing came of it. We have very different expectations out of life."

"Is that it?"

"And I think he wanted me to put in a good word for him." She smiles, but I can hear the hurt hidden in her words.

"Oh, it must hard to be a woman in a high position."

"I'm just a secretary. It hardly counts as a high position."

"You're not just a secretary. You're more

than that. You're my right arm. No, you're both my arms. I wouldn't be where I am today without your help. I'm well aware of the difficulties you've had and I appreciate everything you've done and continue to do for me."

"Jeez, Zane. Did Felicia run some kind of exorcism on you and chase away the demon inside you without you realizing it?"

"Ha ha." I reach out and ruffle her hair, which is loose around her shoulders. "Remind me to fire Tony the first thing Monday. I have no patience with suck-ups who try to use women to climb up the hierarchy."

"You don't have to fire him on my account. He's good at what he does."

I'll probably not fire him right away, but I'll have my eye on him and end his contract on his first failure. Disrespecting someone important to me is a no-go in my book, but I don't need to explain myself to Julie. She should know me by now, plus I don't want to ruin the movie for her.

Our pizza arrives, and we eat it from the box, without bothering to get plates. I drink coke right out of the bottle, too, and offer it to Julie. She takes it from my hands and gulps it down, then quickly realizes her mistake. "Eww, does that mean I kissed Felicia by drinking from the same bottle as you?"

I laugh and grab the bottle out of her hands.

"Did you kiss her on the lips after the deed?" she asks, her eyes narrowed.

I blink, trying to understand her question, then the bulb lights up. She's asking if the bottle has any residuals from my release. If I had kissed Felicia after she blew me, I'd have a taste of my sperm in my mouth and have passed it on to Julie with the bottle of coke.

The idea of smearing Julie's lips with my seed is a turn-on that I have no way to act upon, so I quickly shake my head. "No, I didn't."

She looks away without saying a word, but never again touches the bottle throughout the movie. I assume she finds promiscuous men not charming. Somehow, the thought settles into my stomach like a heavy rock. I put down the pizza slice and pretend to watch the movie while all I'm doing is stealing sideways glances at the concentrated expression on her face.

If I want a solid, stable person as a partner, I should become one before anything else. Maybe it's karma that presents me with women who take sex-related matters lightly. After all, isn't what you give, what you get?

At the end of the movie, I start to get up but notice Julie is asleep, her mouth slightly open and saliva dripping from the corner of her lips. I smile in amusement.

Her head is uncomfortably positioned against the back of the couch, and she'll probably wake up with a neck ache from that position. I consider leaving her that way, but the idea of her being in pain isn't something I can lightly overlook. So, I call her name to wake her. Rather than waking up, she lets out a loud snore. Her face looks hilarious from that angle, so I keep watching her for a minute, then decide to carry her to her bedroom.

She continues sleeping despite the movement when I slip my arms beneath her body and lift her up. She's feather light, but the way she sprawls across the tiny space in my arms with her legs completely exposed makes for an awkward moment as I carry her into her bedroom. Carefully, I lay her on her bed and tuck her under the comforter.

Her hair falls over her face as her head hits the pillow. Tenderly, I push away the thick strands, unable to take my eyes away from the breathtaking beauty of her relaxed features. This isn't lust or physical attraction. This is like watching her inner being, her true self, flash across her face without worry or anger creasing her smooth skin. Her beauty is both calming and purifying.

Suddenly, the feeling of guilt for secretly admiring her tightens my chest. I'm no different than the men who took advantage of her and forced her into dirty sexual acts. She wasn't consenting then, and she's not consenting to my inappropriate admiration now. If awake, there's no way in hell she'd let me in her bedroom to start with.

Quickly, I move away from her bed, not wanting to trespass in her personal space any more than I already have, and start to walk out of her bedroom. Just then, a picture on her nightstand grabs my attention and stops me in my tracks. It's a picture of her with my mother in the garden of our home at the time.

I hold the picture, lifting it up close to my face to see the details. In the background, I'm sitting at a table with Ace and Chloe, playing cards and eating cake. I remember the day. How could I have forgotten it? It was Mom's last birthday, three months before she took her life and left us defenseless in Michael's maniacal hands.

Melancholy and sadness flood my chest. I miss her...her loving hugs, tender voice, even her constant worry over us, her children. But, in this picture, she's staring at the camera with a carefree grin. I can hear my heart cracking in two with pain. She could have lived. She'd finally have had a chance to be truly happy after Michael's death. Why didn't she push through the harsh days and stay with us?

I wish I'd noticed the change in her behavior in those last days before she took the plunge and ended her life. I wish I could have stopped her. A sob pushes up my throat, and I hurriedly set the photo back on the nightstand and rush out of Julie's bedroom.

As I approach the front door of her apartment, I realize I have a problem. The door locks only from the inside, and if I head out and only pull the door behind me, it'll just close, without locking. This is L.A., and in L.A., no residence is safe, if not securely locked. I can look for and find the key to the door, but I'll be locking Julie in her own house. She's screwed if she doesn't have a second key.

Letting out a loud sigh, I push the door closed, turn the lock down, and throw myself on the couch in the living room. I'll have to spend the night on the couch, whether Julie likes my presence in her place or not.

CH 9 - The Breakfast

Since I'll be playing Julie's bodyguard for the night, I might as well enjoy my stay at her place. For me to enjoy myself, I'll need liquor, or else I won't be able to blink an eye tonight with the thoughts of my mother weighing me down.

I search for anything with alcohol in it and only find a half-finished bottle of red wine in the fridge. I gulp the whole damn thing down standing by the fridge and throw the empty bottle in the recycle bin. Everything is clean and neatly organized in Julie's kitchen, including her recycle bin. And I know for a fact she's not the kind of woman to spend her hard-earned money on housemaids. So, she must be spending a huge amount of time cleaning up her home.

While I wait for the alcohol to take its toll on my body and numb me, I go through her DVD collection. She's got several rom-coms, which is to be expected, and also a variety of horror movies, like Lost Highway, The Shining, Rosemary's Baby, and It. Who would have guessed she'd have a dark side to her?

Picking up the Lost Highway DVD, I place it in the player and lie down on the couch. Fortunately, the effect of alcohol blended with the intensity of the movie distracts me enough to push the memories of my mother to the back of my mind, and soon my eyelids feel heavy and I fall asleep.

~

I'm vaguely aware of someone lingering around, but my head throbs with pain, and if my memory doesn't fail me, it's the aftermath of drinking half a bottle of wine way too quickly.

I can't open my eyes just yet, but my ears quickly tune to the faint sounds around me. Slaps of bare feet across the hardwood floor, opening and closing of doors, water running, and low hums of a woman. That woman must be Julie and she must be contemplating my unwelcome sleepover on her couch.

I roll my head to the source of the noise and force my eyes open, only to see Julie biting an apple and wearing nothing but a towel wrapped around her body.

She's not contemplating my sleepover. She's not aware of it at all, which is why she doesn't look bothered when she pushes the edges of the towel between her thighs to dry her intimate parts. Not much of her long, lean legs is left to the imagination as she thoroughly dries herself, while taking big bites of her apple. And at one point, she even bends down to dry her toes and I catch a quick glimpse of her butt cheeks, my eyes ready to jump out of their sockets. Holly heavens!

The sight is disturbing, but also extremely arousing. I should stop eye-fucking her and give her the privacy she thinks she has. As difficult as it feels, I force my eyes to close and pretend to be sleeping. A few minutes pass before I hear a shriek accompanied by a low "Oh, my God!" and something drops on the floor, possibly the apple she's been holding.

My heart races beneath my chest. She knows. She must have figured out I've been peeping. This is worse than a million-dollar lawsuit for sexual harassment, it's simply disrespectful to the woman who has stood by me no matter what.

I should have asked Daney to wait by her door rather than trying to play her bodyguard and majorly failing at it. The only thing she wants protected is her dignity, and I'm stomping all over it with my dirty feet.

I hear her leaving the living room for a few minutes, possibly to put on clothes, and then feel her coming back and hovering over me. This is my cue to open my eyes. I do my absolute best to assure her I've been sleeping the whole time. My eyelids open slowly; I glance around with an obvious look of disorientation. I even make sure to jerk when I move my eyes up to her face.

"Julie, what are you doing here?" I ask with a loud yawn and sit up, rubbing my eyes.

"As far as I'm concerned, this is my condo, and the real question to be asked here is what are you doing here?"

"You fell asleep on the couch. I tried to wake you, but you wouldn't budge. Then I carried you to your bed. I couldn't leave because your door wouldn't lock, so I stayed." I can't help it, my eyes do a quick sweep of her body. She has a pink t-shirt and black yoga tights, which is a turn-off after catching her with just a towel on.

"Oh." Her eyes dart around, her expression uncomfortable. "There's a bed in the guest bedroom."

"I didn't know. That's okay, though. The couch wasn't so bad." The tightening of the muscles around my neck speaks to the contrary, though. I stand and head toward the door. "Since you're awake now and you can lock your door, there's no need for me to stay any longer."

"No. You can't go out like this, looking like hell. Frat House will lose ratings if a photographer catches you in that shape, doing the walk of shame." She motions with her chin toward my wrinkled suit. "Hell, HMG shares will take a massive hit if any living soul with a phone notices you."

Her words inflict panic inside me. A stinky, drunk prick who can't get enough of partying isn't the impression I want to give to the world. "So, what now?"

"Don't worry. I'll call Daney and ask him to bring clean clothes for you. You'll need a razor, too." She runs and quickly grabs her phone off the kitchen island. I chuckle a bit when I listen to her quick, but precise orders to Daney about exactly which suit and shirt he should bring over. As she sets her phone back down on the kitchen island, she grins at me. "All set. Go ahead and have a shower, while I fix you a breakfast. You have two back-to-back dates today, then we're heading to Scarlet's birthday party."

"Oh, that. I should pick out a gift for her."

"Don't worry. I got one for you when I was shopping for mine."

"You're a lifesaver."

"I know." Her gaze falls on the floor, her cheeks blushing a light shade of pink.

I grin and head to the bathroom.

"You can use the fresh towels on the shelves. I'll lay your suit in the guestroom for you," she yells after me.

I take my time in the shower mainly to give Daney time to pick up my clothes so I won't walk around half-naked, wrapped up in a towel. I don't think Julie would accept my indecency as happily as I took hers. That ass of hers! Damn it. Not exactly the visualization I need of her.

My cock hardens with the fresh images of Julie's body in my mind, the warm water caressing my skin only adding to the pleasure. I can't jerk off thinking of Julie. It's as gross as imagining Chloe, my sister, and that's a whole new level of assholeness I don't want to be labeled with, even though no one would know.

Closing my eyes, I force my thoughts toward my last couple of sexual escapades. Felicia and Penelope. The two would make a great team in bed; Felicia sucking me off, Penelope riding my face, while Lindsay and McKenzie making out on the other side of the bed. Now that's an image that has my cock raging hard in a heartbeat.

Covering the head, I start rubbing it in a tight hold. What I need is several women making out and competing to get me off. The taste of pussy, melodic sounds of a climaxing woman, cunts swollen and filled with my come. Why in God's name would I want to give that up for some ungrateful woman whose only pleasure will come from spending my money and nagging me to no end?

The image of McKenzie slipping her fingers inside Lindsay does the trick and makes me jerk a hot load of come into my palm. Breathless, I watch the water wash off my softening cock.

After several times of soaping my body, I decide it's time to get out. With a towel safely wrapped around my hips, I head out of the bathroom, hurry into the guest bedroom down the hall, and smile with satisfaction when I see my clothes neatly laid out on the bed.

"Breakfast is ready!" Julie calls out, the liveliness in her voice pushing a round of old memories of her in our house to the surface of my consciousness. She was always the one gathering us for breakfast. I wouldn't have actually gone down to the kitchen and confronted Michael's evil face if it hadn't been for the cheery conversation Julie provided.

Hastily, I put on my boxers, dress pants and shirt and stroll into the kitchen.

"Spinach-wrapped egg bites?" I yell, widening my eyes to show my surprise and appreciation. "You remember my favorite breakfast dish?"

"Of course I remember." She fills the mugs with coffee and sets them beside the plates. "It wasn't that long ago, was it?"

I try to count the years that must have passed since the days Julie lived with us. "Sixteen, seventeen. That's hell of a long time if you ask me."

She makes a face and pulls up a chair. "That's really long."

"Let's see if you still got it right." I cut a piece of egg with the fork and pop it in my mouth, unable to keep my eyes from rolling at the delectable bite. "Ahh, Julie. Are you trying to give me a heart attack? This food is to die for." I quickly sit on the chair and fork the rest of the entire egg and swallow it down. It's so tasty, it's better than an orgasm.

"Want some more?"

"You have to ask that?"

She puts two more wraps on my plate and watches me gobble them down in a matter of seconds. "You're an animal." She shakes her head as she pushes the entire tray of eggs in front of me.

"This was my mother's favorite, too."

"I know," she states with pride evident in the tone of her voice.

"I saw that you keep a picture of her in your bedroom."

"She'll always have a place in my life."

My lips curl into a pained smile, a lump forming in my throat. Speaking of the past isn't easy and hurts every time. It cuts deep to remember those violent days, the suicide of my mother, the abuse my siblings and I endured at Michael's hands, and the helplessness to do anything about it. Even Julie, herself, had her share of trauma from Michael.

When she first came into our home, she had practically been abandoned. She was the daughter of a successful businessman at that time, but, unfortunately, her father was also Michael's direct competition. Michael managed to push him out of the business and into bankruptcy and finally caused his opponent to die of a brain seizure.

Julie's mother ended up with nothing but debts and a young daughter she didn't really want. Mom ran to help her, lent her money, and volunteered to take care of Julie while Julie's mother found a way to get her life back together. Weeks became months, then years, but her mother never came back to claim her.

I'd hear Julie crying in those early days of moving in with us in the small bedroom Mom arranged for her despite Michael's orders to get rid of her for good. As promised, Mom took good care of her and treated her as if she were one of her own kids. Mom had so much love to give...I can't bear the thought of being deprived of it.

In return, Julie showed Mom unconditional respect and loyalty and stood by her no matter what...even when the day came that she had to pay her debt to Michael. I clearly remember how her eyes sparkled and her face beamed that morning during breakfast. Without Michael around, our breakfasts were magnificent. Mom would cook delicious pastries and eggs for us, and we'd eat and laugh to no end.

Michael came in and told Mom he had to take Julie to a doctor's appointment. Mom looked concerned and tried her best to keep Julie safe from Michael's twisted plans. When the day was over and Michael brought Julie back, her liveliness had vanished, and the sparkle in her eyes had perished. Her cry-filled nights returned and she never returned to being that hopeful girl she once had been.

My appetite diminishes on the spot, but I eat two more eggs out of courtesy, all the while keeping my eyes fixed on my plate so Julie won't notice the change in my mood.

"This was wonderful," I compliment her and take my dish to the sink. "Thanks for having me over," I say and quickly head for the door before she can distract me.

"I'll text you the information about your dates," she reminds me while standing by the door as I stroll to the elevator.

"Thanks."

"See you at the party?"

"Yeah."

CH 10 - JULIE - The Goodbye

I was only twelve when my mother kissed my cheek on a cold rainy day and told me she had to go and that I'd have to stay with another family for a while. She placed my hand into Irene's and gave me a reassuring smile, although her blue eyes were filled with tears.

"She'll take care of you, but in return you'll have to do what she says." Taking a step away from me, she adjusted her black scarf and long black coat around her small and slim body. Raindrops sparkled on her short brown hair and pale skin.

I refused to look at Irene and kept my eyes firmly on my mother. I was angry and confused. I didn't understand what was going on. I'd had babysitters staying with me when my parents went out. And I certainly didn't see what the big deal about Irene was.

"We'll have lots of fun together." Irene knelt before me to put herself on my eyelevel and squeezed my hand gently in hers. "I have a daughter your age. She's always wanted a sister." Her warm brown eyes shimmered when she gazed at me with a nurturing glance that promised safety and care. Her smile was genuine and the only thing that kept me from bursting into tears of anger.

My mother cleared her throat, and with one glance at her, I knew she was uncomfortable. "I won't be gone for long," she said in a low voice.

"I know." Irene straightened and opened her handbag with her free hand, slipping out a thick envelope. "This should cover everything you need."

My mother clasped the envelope with both hands and quickly examined its contents. "Thank you," were the last words I heard from her before she slid into the back seat of a taxi and took off.

I waved after her, resisting the urge to cry

as the taxi disappeared among the other vehicles on the busy street. She'd come back to pick me up. She always did. My worries were in vain.

I looked up at Irene and forced myself to smile. Different from my other babysitters, she lifted my hand and placed a kiss on the back of it. Her kiss felt good and helped me relax, although I still worried about my mother and when she'd pick me up.

Irene wasn't lying about having a daughter—Chloe. She was remarkably beautiful and had many nice clothes and toys, but she rarely smiled. I didn't understand why she wasn't happy. Her mom hadn't left her with some stranger and she owned everything a child could dream off.

Her two brothers weren't much different in terms of gloominess, either. They usually kept to themselves in their bedrooms when their father was at home. When he wasn't, now that was a reason to celebrate.

Michael was a stern man who didn't know the meaning of a genuine smile. He made sure I knew he despised my presence in his home and even told me to my face to "fuck off" more than once. I feared him to the extent that I couldn't talk in his presence. I couldn't even move when he was around. I was afraid one night, while everyone was asleep, he'd take me out of my bed, drag me out, and leave me alone in the woods.

I fiercely willed my mother to come and take me back. My heartbeat would race when there was a knock on the front door, my hopes high that the visitor would be my mother. She'd wrap her arms around me, press me into her warm body, and whisper to me that the time had come to go back home.

I waited and waited...watched out of the window of my new bedroom for a taxi, shedding tears into my new pillow in the night while praying to have her back the following day.

The memories of her and my father slowly began to fade, and I hated myself for starting to forget the details of her face. Despite my grief, I enjoyed my new family. Chloe was mostly silent and into herself, but once she warmed up to me, we became best friends. Zane tried to ignore me for most of the first three years of my stay with them, but whenever I had a problem, he'd leave everything and run to my rescue. Ace was the lonely soul of the family, and Irene tended him relentlessly.

I loved each and every one of them, but loving someone comes with a price. And the price is, hurting with them when they were hurt. My heart bled for them when Michael mercilessly punished their young bodies, slashing their tender souls. He was a maniac, a demon disguised as a human.

He punished Chloe with uncountable strokes of his belt until she passed out from pain for simply inviting a classmate to her birthday party, who happened to be a boy. The embarrassment she endured lasted long after the scars on her body had healed. She was banned from talking to boys. She couldn't so much as glance at one. And when Zane or Ace tried to interfere with Michael's cruel punishment of her, they were rewarded with double the amount of Chloe's punishment.

To me, he was a real murderer, because he killed his children alive. He denied them a happy and decent life and sucked out their souls and their joy of living.

He didn't touch me, though. After he realized that Irene wouldn't give up on me, he simply ignored me and carried on with his life as if I'd never existed.

Until one day he told me I needed to do something for him.

Irene didn't believe him when he said he was taking me to the doctor. She stood between him and the door to block his way. "You're not taking her anywhere," she shouted, despite knowing all too well how he reacted to being yelled at.

He merely gripped her arms and shoved her to the side, signaling me with his head to go ahead.

Irene hit the side table and nearly fell. "No," she shouted behind me and grabbed Michael by his elbow to stop him, and I stood paralyzed at the doorway, unable to take my eyes from the train wreck taking place before me. Something was terribly wrong, or Irene wouldn't try so hard to stop him, endangering her wellbeing and that of her children.

Michael pushed her away so hard, she fell

headfirst to the floor, both Zane and Ace jumping to her side to help her up. Taking advantage of their panic, Michael ushered me out and into his car.

While his driver drove the car, Michael fished an envelope out of his briefcase and handed it to me without speaking. Curious and my heart fluttering, I opened the envelope and pulled some documents and a picture out of it, gazing at them with a questioning look. The photo was an image of a woman, who looked very much like my mother, with a hospital gown on.

"Your mother is sick," Michael said briefly and pointed at the picture in my hand. "Skin cancer. She needs money for her treatment."

It'd been so long since I'd heard anything about my mother, Michael's words caught me off-guard and punched the air out of my lungs. "Where is she?"

"Doesn't matter. In a hospital in Boston, fighting for her life."

I dared shift my gaze from the picture and lift my eyes to Michael's face. "Can I see her?"

He glanced down at me and, for the first time, there was no indifference or anger in his eyes. "No, but you can save her life."

"How?"

"I'll explain how to you in a moment."

He didn't speak for the rest of the drive while I tried to make sense of the medical terms on the papers in my hands. Stage 4 Melanoma. Cancerous cells metastasized to local lymph node. Biopsy. Chemotherapy. Surgery. Medical fees for recommended surgery and follow-up treatment: $150,000.00.

I was only sixteen by that time and the most money I'd ever had at one time was a twenty dollar bill. I didn't have a clear concept of how much $150,000.00 was, but I knew only a handful of people could afford it, and my mother wasn't one of them.

I was heartbroken over being abandoned, but I didn't want her to suffer. I was ready to accept anything Michael wanted from me so she could recover. I missed her terribly, although I didn't remember much of her after so many years of being away from her, except for the comfort I'd felt in her arms, listening to her soothing words. I wished she hadn't gone away. I wished things had been different and I still had both my mother and father.

I couldn't help the tears streaming down my cheeks as the car pulled in front of a building that looked like a hotel. Even though I didn't have the slightest idea what we were doing there, I followed Michael through the reception area and into the elevator.

"Stop crying," he whispered once the elevator doors closed, his voice devoid of any emotion. "You'll save your mother. She'll live. I've got the best doctors in the country treating her."

"Thank you!" I wiped my tears away, clutching the envelope holding my mother's diagnosis and picture.

"You don't need to thank me. You're going to earn the money for her medical expenses yourself."

"How?" I looked up at him for an answer, but he kept his eyes on the elevator doors and didn't open his mouth until he and I stood in a luxury suite. "I need you to listen to me carefully." He pulled me down to a couch and sat next to me, staring directly into my eyes. "You're a beautiful girl...innocent and sweet. You'll use that to save your mother. I have a business associate interested in you. He's ready to pay whatever it takes to have you."

My heart sank into my stomach. I was sixteen, still a child.

"It's only for a couple of hours, then I'll wire the money to the hospital where your mother is a patient. She'll have her surgery today, as soon as they have the expenses paid up front."

"But, I have never had...sex before."

"That's kind the whole point, darling. Think about your mother. You're her only chance. She'll die very soon if she doesn't get the surgery."

I swallowed hard, trying to catch my breath and think a way out of this puzzle. She'd left me, hadn't even contacted me, and now I had to surrender myself to a pervert so she could have a chance to live. Life wasn't fair. "I can't do it."

"You can't? If your mother dies, which she will if she doesn't get the surgery immediately, do you think you can continue living? Knowing she could have survived, but you were too selfish to help her? You won't get another chance like this. If you turn down the offer now, my associate won't be begging you to spread your legs. He'll just move on to the next available virgin. You'll not earn anything out of it, and your mother will die in a matter of days. Is that what you want?"

The cruelty in his words had me crying hard into my hands. Of course I didn't want my mother to die, no matter how she had treated me.

A knock on the door startled me.

"Go to the bathroom to wash up and don't come out until I say so." Michael stood, pointing to the bathroom, and strode to the door.

Closing the bathroom door behind me, I stood in the dark for a moment to listen to the conversation taking place on the other side. It was hard to make out the words. It didn't take a genius to guess what they could be talking about. Probably sorting out the details of the indecent agreement.

I turned on the lights and took a long look at myself, trying to engrave in my mind every little detail of my appearance before losing my innocence at the hands of a pervert. For being in my situation, I looked unusually calm, save for the tears rolling down my cheeks.

I washed my face with cold water and ordered myself to stop crying right that second. I could be giving myself to a man for the first time, but I wouldn't give anyone the pleasure of seeing me crying and vulnerable.

My eyes were still red when I dried my face with a hand towel. I breathed in and out slowly, telling myself this was for my mother, that her health was more important than a few hours of discomfort.

I wasn't nervous anymore when the bathroom door opened after a soft knock. Michael stood in the doorway, his face revealing no emotion. "I'll wait for you down at reception."

He watched me step out of the bathroom and squeezed my shoulder with a gentle hold before stalking out of the suite. Without allowing myself to think, I took slow steps toward the bedroom and pushed open the door.

The man who had paid thousands of dollars for my virginity stood by the king-sized bed and turned his head toward me as I stepped in. A sickening smile curved his mouth, and the repulsive sweep of his eyes over my body turned my stomach upside down.

I knew him. Irene had invited him and his family over for dinner a couple of times. He had two daughters about my age. He'd asked me how school was going, and if I had any hobbies. How could he think of me that way?

He sat on the bed and patted it in invitation. "Hello, Julie."

My stomach wouldn't give me a rest. I couldn't push away the disgusting thoughts of his hands and lips all over me. I couldn't even walk toward him, how was I supposed to spend hours in the same bed with him?

"Come sit next to me." He patted on the bed once again, this time quicker.

My heart thudded harder against my chest as my feet followed his order and walked toward the bed. I sat beside him, folding my hands in my lap, my eyes locked on the floor.

"I know you're nervous, but I promise I'll be gentle."

Now, that's a relief. How about you leave me alone and find a whore who's willing to fulfill your wishes without being forced to.

"You're so beautiful." He moved closer and covered my hands in my lap. "And that dress you were wearing during the last dinner... I just couldn't help myself."

Now it was my fault. I shouldn't have been wearing a dress. I should have had something decent to protect my dignity from preying eyes. Now it was too late. There was no going back to that evening, nor to the moment my mother had given me away. If I'd know this was how I would end up, I'd have wrapped myself around my mother's waist and never let her go.

CH 11 - The Lawyer

Daisy's is a high-profile restaurant where actors and agents hang out more often than any other professional group, and surprisingly, it's also the location Julie picked for my date with Ashley, an immigration lawyer based in downtown L.A. I don't know where Ashley lives, but if it's anywhere around downtown, she'll need an hour's drive to get here, more so with the weekend traffic.

The waitress welcomes me by my name and walks me to a table out on the terrace, where daisies and lilacs hang down on every corner. Several heads turn as I navigate through the tables, a few of them familiar. I nod to those who smile at me and settle at the table the waitress shows me.

"What can I get you?" the waitress asks with a smile.

"Vodka on the rocks."

"Zane, my friend!" A man cheers from behind me and hands grab my shoulders.

Merlin Angeli, an agent I've known and been friends with for many long years. I immediately stand to shake hands, both of us laughing at the opportunity to meet since our last contact a year ago. After small talk about the entertainment business, I ask him who he's with.

He signals with his hand toward a table by the door. "With the beautiful Brandy Benfield."

I work hard to keep the disgust off my face as I wave at Brandy, who shouts a flirty "Hello," at me. I can smell her desperation from a mile away.

She's one of those one-hit wonders, who by luck, snatched a big role in a blockbuster, then vanished into obscurity after being unable to handle the sudden fame. In other words, she started acting as if her shit didn't stink and treated everyone around her like a piece of garbage while expecting the red carpet to be rolled out for her left and right.

When she realized there was no shortage of pretty faces and double DDs in Hollywood, it was too late for her, and her pitiful attempts to grab roles by spreading her legs to every producer with an upcoming project gained her nothing but a bad name.

I feel puke rising in my throat as I remember the night I spent with her, although she was down to do anything I wanted, including anal and threesome play. At that time, I wasn't aware her eagerness was out of pure desperation to get her name back on the big screen. She played the innocent with a brilliant persuasiveness, I must give her that. But, the word about her desperation got around fast, and I cut all contact with her before she could take advantage of me.

I respond to Brandy's eager wave with a quick nod of my head to prevent her from inviting herself over to my table and turn my attention back to Merlin. "I'll see you around."

It must be my lucky day because right at that time, Ashely, my date, emerges from the doorway. I recognize her from the photo Julie sent me along with the intensive background information she gathered about her.

When our eyes meet, Ashley smiles and quickly swings through the tables. I can't keep my eyes from sweeping her curvy yet firm body up and down. A red halter dress is tastefully clinging to her tall figure, and the sexuality oozing out of her immediately pushes away any disgusting thoughts from my past.

Her beauty captivates my mind in a heartbeat. Her hair is a darker shade of blonde, her lips full and seductive, her eyes lit with joy, her skin dark and smooth. She's the carbon copy of Beyoncé, except for her short hair. I can picture our beautiful babies, a half dozen of them, because as attractive as she is, there's no way I'll be able to take a break from knocking her up.

I grab her hand and raise it to my lips to get a quick taste of the skin I'll hopefully soon be devouring. I might have lost my appetite after Felicia's speedy blowjob, but Ashley's beauty is extraordinary, I'll give her extra points if she intends to suck my dick within the next twenty-four hours. Yeah, I'm a hypocrite like that. Sue me.

"Hello, Zane. What a pleasure to meet you." She approaches me with an air of natural confidence. Her beautiful smile widens, revealing her pearly whites.

"The pleasure is definitely mine, and I assure you this is the first time I really mean it."

She laughs at my comment, her cheeks turning pink, and gently slides her hand out of my hold. I notice the male guests at the neighboring tables shooting me jealous glances when I pull a chair out for Ashley. Even Merlin lifts an eyebrow in my direction.

Ashley is a solid twelve on an attractiveness scale of ten. And that alone has me drooling for her. And as if that's not enough, she happens to be a brilliant lawyer with a summa cum laude from U.C.L.A.! There's no way I'm letting her go. That's why I put on my A game and play the perfect gentleman.

"I've never had a blind date before," she confesses as we sip our vodkas. "In fact, I don't have time to go on dates. My assistant set up my online dating profile. I'm not really sure what she wrote about me."

"I think your assistant deserves a raise in salary. I'm grateful to have the chance the get to know you." I set down my glass and shoot her a long, seductive look. I allow my blood to flow between my legs, hardening my cock just enough to feel testosterone running through my veins. Women can sense it when a man is aroused and ready to take them. It heightens their awareness and interest, although they probably have no idea why.

She responds with a sharp breath of air and licks her lips, her expression turning serious. "I...I...thank you."

I grin to ease her tension. "So, tell me about your work."

"I help undocumented immigrants who face deportation unite with their children," she starts with a practiced ease. "When illegal immigrants are detained or arrested by the police, their children are transferred to foster care. The detention centers don't allow parents to be at the court hearings to regain custody of their children. It's nearly impossible to meet the requirements of the child welfare system from jail anyway. If not helped, the parents lose custody of their children for good."

Now that's a good cause. "That sounds horrible."

"Yeah. We do the best we can. We're a new firm, only two years old, but so far we've helped a few dozen families reunite."

"I'm impressed." And intrigued by her success.

"We still have a long way to go. There're thousands of families who need legal help. Maybe you should consider making a movie about this issue to raise awareness."

"Only if you'll star as the main character." I wink at her and watch with amazement as she melts and turns her eyes down to the table in embarrassment. "I assume your work keeps you very busy," I say in an attempt to change the topic to a lighter subject.

"Yeah, it's true, but I manage to spare time for my hobbies. I love surfing and gardening. I go to the movies and bowling. I swim and do yoga regularly. There's no shortage of time for those who like to play, right?"

"That's indeed true. Have you ever thought of marrying and settling down?" Even though the question makes me feel like I'm interviewing Ashley, I can see Julie smiling at it in approval.

"I've always wanted a family with two kids. It's just that the dating scene is intimidating. It's hard to see if a man is serious or just playing the game to get laid. But, what's written about you isn't exactly hope-inducing."

I laugh hard at her forwardness. "I won't lie and deny my womanizer tendencies," I admit after I can get my laughter in check. "I'm guilty of loving women a bit too much. But I know a catch when I see one, and you, my dear, aren't just a catch, you're a keeper."

She narrows her eyes at me, her brows furrowing for quite a long time, as she judges my honesty. "I might be a keeper, but your observation doesn't say anything about your willingness to get serious."

I straighten up, squaring my shoulders, erasing the playful laughter off my lips. "I'm ready to settle down for the right woman," I say with my most earnest voice.

Looking content with my answer, she starts talking about her retired parents, her two sisters who own a ranch just outside of Glenwood, her high school sweetheart who died in a car accident two weeks into their engagement, her three-legged Spaniel roommate, and her four-bedroom home she bought last year by the Grove but hasn't started decorating yet.

From the details she reveals about herself and the way she talks, I can tell she comes from a loving home and that she's humane, vulnerable, sometimes silly, yet smart without being pretentious, which is hard to find in the entertainment world. In short, her character and beauty leave me speechless, and I desperately hope my impression of her won't be ruined as in Felicia's case.

After the waitress clears out our dishes, Ashley gives me a quizzical look, asking me 'what's next?' without using words. I can't just let her go, so I request the waitress to bring us menus so we can order dessert. Ashley lets out a long breath and scans the menu quickly. We order strawberry cheesecake and dessert wine to go with it and continue our lively conversation while waiting for our orders.

When the waitress returns with our dessert, I mentally start to lay out a plan to keep Ashley's attention. A woman with her beauty, brains, and sweetness is a rare occurrence, and I'd be a fool if I ruined the chance to get to know her better. The day is still young, and L.A. has several romantic spots I can take her to without intimidating her. A friendly stroll by the sea in Santa Monica, a quick visit to LACMA. Even Lake Hollywood is only forty minutes away and the drive there in my limousine will give me more time to indulge myself in her beauty.

Just when I decide on my next move, a gentle grab of a hand on my shoulder stops me before I can move forward with my plan, and what I see makes me cringe. Literally cringe with disappointment and anger.

Brandy Benfield leans down to give me an intimate kiss on the cheek and slides her goddamn hand possessively from one shoulder to the other. "Hello Zane. I should actually be mad at you for making yourself scarce after that night we spent at your condo, but I can't. You're too sexy to be mad at," she says with what I assume is meant to be a cute, childish voice, but it only sounds like chair legs scraping the floor. Then, she turns to Ashley. "He's always been like that, hot in the beginning, cold after he gets what he wants."

Ashley's good mood deteriorates instantly and blood abandons the smooth skin of her beautiful face. Her eyes move from Brandy to me, her gaze revealing her disappointment.

"I'm sorry for my manners. I'm Brandy Benfield." Brandy shoves her hand toward Ashley to shake hands, pushing her hip against the side of my body in the process.

"I watched Falling Apart at least five times." Ashley takes Brandy's hand in a professional manner, her voice warm despite the cold expression on her face. "It's a beautiful story."

"Thank you, sweetheart," Brandy says in her condescending voice as she looks down at me. "She's gorgeous. Let me know if you're up for a threesome, like we did last time with that eighteen-year-old striptease." A naughty and knowing laughter punctuates the most embarrassing words ever uttered about me.

Here's a smart, beautiful, loving woman worthy of any man's commitment, but I can't stop her from slipping through my fingers. Worst of it all, Brandy isn't coming up with a fake story. I indeed fucked her and an eighteen-year-old striptease at my condo and it wasn't even all that long ago.

I can't speak, neither can Ashley, while we look at each other with shock. After dropping her carefully planted bomb, Brandy releases me from her hold and wishes us a great rest of the day, not skipping the opportunity to plaster her dirty lips on my cheek before she leaves.

Ashley's chest rises with a deep intake of air as she reaches for her purse to get money out. "This was a lovely meal. Unfortunately, I have to get back to work." She places a hundred dollar bill beside her glass, and I know exactly what she's trying to convey with her gesture. Women, especially the high-quality ones, don't like feeling in debt when there's no chance for a second date, and after Brandy's reveal, no worthy woman would waste time on a follow-up date with me.

Feeling angry at myself, I launch forward and capture her hand. "Please, stay."

Her shimmering black eyes glance back at me with sadness. "There's no reason for me to stay unless what she said about you and a barely legal striptease was a lie."

"It's true, and I'm very ashamed of it."

"Hmm." Slowly, she slides her hand away from beneath mine and closes her bag. "That's unfortunate."

"It is. But it was in the past. I'm not interested in that life anymore. I'm looking forward to dedicating myself to one woman only, and I wish you could give me a chance to prove that to you."

She shakes her head, looking unconvinced by my declaration. "Past behavior is a reliable predictor of future behavior. I can't waste my limited time on something so predictably unfulfilling. I'm sorry, but you're not the type of man I'm planning to get involved with."

"Ashley, please."

"I'm sorry." She gets to her feet with a clear conviction and strides through the tables into the restaurant building.

I gaze at the door, hating myself for ruining a perfectly good opportunity with my shameful past. Julie was right. I don't have the right to demand a high-quality woman when my past is nothing but appalling. The women I want won't want me, and those who want me aren't exactly marriage material. My quest for a happy family life is looking less promising all the time. So, where does that leave me?

CH 12 - The Unreachable

My phone rings as I walk out of the restaurant, disappointment at losing the chance to get to know Ashley due to my promiscuous lifestyle still heavy on my chest. Ignoring the curious looks on the passers-by on the street, I place the phone against my ear.

"How was it?" Julie shouts enthusiastically on the other line.

"Terrible. Brandy Benfield was there."

"Oh, my God! Brandy of all people. She's such a gossip."

"She's more than a gossip. She spilled all my dirty laundry to Ashley. So disappointing. Ashley was a catch."

Her voice comes off even more cheerful

when she says, "Don't you worry about it. Next on the list is even better."

"I highly doubt it. I don't know how you managed to find her, but she was a precious diamond. I don't think I'll find another woman like her."

Julie gives me the address for the next date, which is another restaurant only two blocks away. I look left and right over my shoulders to make sure Brandy isn't around to eavesdrop and sabotage my next date.

Unbeknownst to Julie, this back-to-back date arrangement was actually a great idea, because meeting another woman is the only way to help me get over my humiliating failure. Although it's hard to say goodbye to Ashley, my next date will be my rescue.

I arrive twenty minutes early for my next date and order red wine while waiting and mentally preparing myself for another woman.

Soren is thirty, of Danish origin, and the founder of an online clothing boutique. From the photo Julie attached of her, she could easily be a supermodel with her tall, lean figure and long pale-blonde hair. Julie clearly knows my weakness for blonde women, including the dyed blondes.

I sip my drink slowly, passing the time reading and re-reading the lines on Soren's resume. I'm on my fourth glass of wine when my phone rings again with Julie's call.

"Zane, I just received a call from Soren, your date. She can't make it."

"Figures."

"She asked if she can reschedule it."

I roll my eyes in slight anger. "Sure."

"Three weeks from today?"

"What? That's too long. I can wait here another hour if she can make it."

"No. She has to fly to Dubai in two hours and won't be back until Saturday in three weeks. Oh, wait, you have to be in New York that Saturday. Hold on. I'll call her secretary to arrange another date... Hey... Her secretary just told me Soren has a flight scheduled for that Saturday afternoon to Columbia. Her next open date is in six weeks. What do you say?"

"What do I say?" I repeat with sarcasm. "Tell her that I don't have time for a woman who can't make time for me."

"Are you angry?" Julie asks, her voice tender with compassion.

"Not at you," I say apologetically. "At myself."

"I'm sorry things didn't work out as you planned. I have several other dates lined up for you. You'll find the woman who'll make you happy when the time is right. I promise."

"I give up. I'm not exactly a family guy. I know myself, I won't change from night to day. I am who I am and I was happy that way until you came up with your marriage scheme. Sorry Julie, but it won't work." I disconnect before she can try and convince me to the contrary. My shoulders slumped, I order the waitress to bring me the whole bottle of wine. I might as well toast the return to my bachelor life.

CH 13 - JULIE - Dirty Love

All is fair in love and war.

Isn't that what common belief holds? I might have done certain things that I'm not proud of. I might have lied, manipulated, and misinformed some individuals along the way. But, it's all fair because the main purpose behind every little, wicked move I've made is winning his love. Zane's heart.

So what if I told Felicia that Zane would never consider a woman romantically if she wasn't down for blowing him on the first date. I thought she'd back off and change her mind. After all, she was a devoted Christian. But she was okay with the idea. Although I must say I wasn't shocked at her willingness to get Zane's attention, it's Zane we're talking about. A high-end prostitute or a virgin, any girl would want to call him hers.

Ashley was my best candidate. If anyone on my list had a chance to be called Mrs. Zane Hawkins, it was her. She was smart, beautiful, exotic, dedicated and very feminine. I know Zane well enough to know he'd lose his mind over her in a matter of seconds. That's why I had to up my game. She wouldn't accept my suggestions, anyway.

The gossips about Brandy Benfield's hopeless attempts at landing a role—any role—basically fell into my lap. I made a few calls around and found out about her lunch date with Merlin at Daisy's. I didn't have the slightest doubt she wouldn't be able to keep her big mouth shut and would ruin Zane's date. She'd bragged about the one and only night she'd fooled Zane into sleeping with her for months on end, she wouldn't so easily forget it or allow anyone else, including Zane, to forget it, either.

Poor Zane. I wish I could see how sour his face got when Brandy blurted out, possibly proudly, the details of their night together. He'd hate me if he knew about my role in ruining his date, but at its core, it's his fault. He's the one who beds anything with a hole, not me.

Soren wasn't a big deal. She's a businesswoman and I appealed to that side of her. Being busy while climbing up the career leader is understandable. Couple that with the little lie I made up about Zane's appreciation of a woman who's unattainable, and I could convince her to be super greedy with her schedule. The result: immediate dismissal from a possible date with Zane.

I have plans for each and every candidate on the list. I told Nora, a third year resident at Cedar Sinai, to exaggerate the number of men she'd slept with. Turns out, she didn't need to exaggerate anything. Her number, a whopping 237, is enough to turn even the most desperate man off. How she found time to study for med school and survive the night shifts at the hospital is beyond me, not to mention the variety of STD's her vagina must be hosting. Yikes.

I suggested that Elizabeth, a PhD candidate in Etymology, come clean about the three abortions she'd had within the last two years.

The list goes on. I have plans for every one of the seventeen ladies left on the list. I will make sure Zane meets them all and hates them all. And if he requests me to find him more women, I will. But, I will make sure every one has a reason to be dismissed. That's the game. That's my plan to make him realize no woman will be good enough for him, save for yours truly.

What I feel for him isn't an obsession. I understand his needs better than anyone else. I can read his thoughts just from a look on his face. I can see the scars in his soul. I know him like the back of my hand. If I find there's another woman who can give him true happiness, I'll gladly hand him over to her, but such a woman doesn't exist. He believed Lindsay was the one, but she never loved him in the first place.

Speaking of Lindsay, it turns out she's not the opportunist latching onto wealthy men in the hopes to get on the gravy train, I thought she was. She's actually a fairly decent girl and thanks to her eagle eyes, she noticed my crush on Zane early on. Ever since she found out about my secret, we've become good friends, and she's the only one who knows my secret plan to get Zane.

Gripping my phone tightly in my palm, I turn to Lindsay. "Ashley is out. Soren didn't even stand a chance."

"How many left on the list?" She pours herself another cup of coffee and reaches for the cookies on the plate on my kitchen counter.

"Seventeen."

Her eyes grow large in surprise as she takes a bite from one of the chocolate chip cookies I baked for her this morning when she'd told me she'd stop by. Something must be going on in Lindsay-ville. I can tell by the sheer number of cookies she's gulped down since she walked in half an hour ago.

"Why did you pick so many women? He'll screw them all. Is that what you want?" she asks.

A fair question that has me thinking. Of course, I hate to think of Zane in another woman's arms, but I have to focus on the end game. It doesn't matter how many soldiers I'll lose in the battle as long as I have the victory in the end.

"I'm just hoping he'll come to his senses before he has to go through the entire list." I eye the cookie plate with longing. I love cooking and baking, but more than anything I love eating. However, I need to stay in shape and those cookies are just obstacles on my way to happiness. That's why I try to take pleasure from feeding friends and colleagues.

"This is Zane we're talking about. He won't come to his senses as long as there's an available vagina waiting for him."

"That's crass." I cringe at her words, more so because she's right.

"Zane is crass."

"What would you recommend then?"

She shrugs and pointedly glances at my clothes. "Make yourself a little bit more available."

I gulp, feeling a cold shiver running down my spine, and cross an arm across my torso. "What do you mean?"

"You know...your clothes."

"What's wrong with my clothes?"

"They're too depressing. You look like a walking funeral."

I force myself to smile despite the discomfort settling heavily in the pit of my stomach. I'm well aware of the impression I give off with my clothes. The first thing I did after Michael's death was to get rid of all the revealing clothes he forced me to wear while working for him, but it seems my choice of wardrobe might be as much of an obstacle as those cookies.

"What do you suggest?" I'm curious about her observation, but there's no way I'm going back to skirts riding high on my thighs, either.

She walks around me, assessing me with a laser-focused stare from head to toe, making hmm, hmm sounds while thinking. "You're a brunette with a light complexion."

I smile at her comment. "Doesn't take a scientist to figure that out."

"Your neck is a little too long and your shoulders are a bit on the narrow side."

I reach for my neck, covering it with my hand, feeling unsettled by her not-so-flattering observations.

"Your hips could be curvier," she continues, still making circles around my body." "And your legs longer."

"Can you please stop pointing out my flaws?"

Stopping before me, she takes a deep breath, grinning. "That's all. Now we should get you clothes to cover those flaws and flatter your body shape. Can I take a look at your wardrobe?"

"By all means." I head to my bedroom and let her in.

She opens the closet and goes through my clothes one by one, although I know she won't find anything useful in there. I can't see myself putting on anything useful according to her definition, anyway. So this conversation is actually a waste of time, but she's a friend and I should let her try to help me.

"Sorry to say this, but your taste in clothes is horrible." Her eyes move from my dark-colored suits on the hangers to the black jeans I'm wearing along with a black cotton shirt. She picks up a black pants suit and wrinkles her nose as if she's holding a piece of garbage. "Uhhh! Seriously, you don't have any summer dresses? Men love dresses. All of them. It's a universal fact. We need to go shopping right now."

"I'm not exactly a dress type of girl," I confess uncomfortably and lean against the door frame.

"You used to have lots of them. What happened to that sexy red dress you wore at Michael's party?"

"I gave it away along with the other revealing clothes."

"Why?" Her voice is deep and raspy, her gaze demanding.

"I need to make some phone calls for Scarlet's birthday party tonight," I say in an effort to change the subject, as it reminds me of the painful past, and I'd rather erase those memories permanently. "I'm getting the cake for her."

"Just tell me why you gave away your clothes." She hangs the pants-suit she was holding back its place and takes a step toward me. Then abruptly, she stops in her tracks, her eyes growing large with realization. "Is it because...?" Her jaw drops and her mouth pops open. "I'm so sorry. I didn't realize. I'm a horrible person."

I look away, the pain tightening my stomach, the memories of being forced to please other men hitting me hard. An unexpected sob shakes my body, hopefully not visibly. "You're not," I manage to say.

"Yes, I am. You should be able to wear whatever makes you feel comfortable, and if Zane doesn't see your true beauty, it's his loss."

I shrug and swallow the painful lump in my throat. "That would be wishful thinking. You were right in your earlier assessment. I need to do something about my wardrobe. I need to look more appealing. Men are visual creatures, and Zane is even more so."

Her glossy pink lips curl up with an understanding smile. Closing the distance between us, she rubs my upper arm with a gentle stroke of her hand. "You don't have to wear slutty clothes. There're several options where you can look cute and sensual without revealing half your body."

She's right. With Michael, I was only allowed to wear scanty dresses, and now long skirts and shabby jackets are all I have. There must be a middle ground. "I'm gonna need your help shopping for an outfit for Scarlet's party."

Piling my phone and keys into a handbag, I follow Lindsay outside. When behind the wheel of her car, she glances at her phone with sad eyes, her long sigh leading me to wonder if she's going through hard times in her relationship. Although Ace seems crazy in love with Lindsay, he's from an unstable family and might not know exactly how to interpret Lindsay's emotions.

"Is everything okay?" I ask with a friendly smile.

Lifting her gaze up from her phone, she gives her head a quick shake and inserts the key into the ignition. "No. Not really, but I don't want to talk about it."

As the car merges into traffic, my handbag vibrates with an incoming call, and I fish out my phone to see Cary's name blaring on the screen. The screenwriter I'm trying to convince Zane to hire is a kind man and very hardworking. "Hi Cary, how is everything going?"

"Great. Just wanted to let you know about the screenplay I've written for the upcoming episode." His voice trembles as the last words roll out of his mouth. His shyness is a fresh breath of air among the very confident and extroverted people in Hollywood.

"Really. Are you telling me you put together a complete screenplay for the next episode? Not just jotting down a few ideas?" In just a day?

"Yeah, I'm just grateful for the opportunity, you know. The show is fantastic. I can't wait to be part of it."

"Great." I grin in satisfaction. If only I can land another writer with his creativity and enthusiasm, the show will rise to new heights in terms of ratings. "Send me over the script. I'll take a look at it today."

"Sounds fantastic. I'm looking forward to hearing what you think about it."

I hang up and go right to my inbox. A new email pops up, and I upload the word file to glance through it.

"Is it about Frat House?" Lindsay asks while waiting on the red light. "Is Conner going to jail? But, no. Don't tell me! I'll just find it out Thursday. It's fucking killing me, though."

My grin widens in satisfaction. Lindsay is behaving no different than the rest of the millions of Frat House audience; treating the characters of the show as if they're real. That's exactly why the show needs strong writers. "Have you heard of Henrietta Cruz?"

"Yeah, from Troubled Girls, right?"

"You know her? Did you watch the show?"

"Not obsessively. It was fun in the beginning, then the story started repeating itself. Sheela loses her job and gets into depression in the first season, then the same thing happens to Francie's husband in the third season. Why repeat the same thing? Like they can't come up with a different story or something."

"That's true." That again coincides with Henrietta's participation in the writers' team. She probably didn't care about the first season's storyline. I must find a way to make Zane understand she's not a good fit for the team. Just one more thing on my list of things I want Zane to understand.

CH 14 - JULIE - The Makeover

After three hours of non-stop shopping, Lindsay and I finally find a suitable dress that I can wear without feeling like a slut and that Lindsay deems sexy enough. It's a dark-pink, knee-length sheath dress with long sleeves. Lindsay insists I should skip wearing a bra beneath it and shakes her head dismissively when I try it on with one.

"You're actually drawing more attention to your chest with a bra," she says when I put on the dress once again back at home.

"Really?" I study my reflection through the mirror in my bedroom. My boobs appear huge beneath the tight dress. "Jesus, you're right. I'll have to put on a cardigan."

"Please, no! You're gonna ruin a perfectly

good dress with a cardigan." Going through the shoes hanging on the wall inside my wardrobe, she picks out black pumps and hands them to me. "Just wear these and nothing else."

I slide into the high heels, while my eyes are still locked on my unbelievably large chest. I don't even have big breasts, only B-cup, but thanks to the body-hugging style of the dress, especially around the waist, my boobs could easily be mistaken for a C-cup.

"You look gorgeous. You'll blow his mind." Lindsay covers her wide-open mouth with both hands, her eyes gleaming brightly as they sweep over my body. I can't say I'm bothered by her enthusiasm, but if, as a girl, she thinks I'm gorgeous, what will the men on the street think?

"Are you sure?" I hesitate to turn to the side and examine how much bigger my ass looks in this tight dress, but the sight isn't half as terrible as I've expected.

"Yes! I'm absolutely sure. Come on. Let's get your hair and makeup done, too."

I glance down at my watch. Only half an hour before the party starts and I still have to get the birthday cake from the bakery. After a quick shower, I pull the chair before the vanity and let Lindsay style my hair and do my makeup. When she's done and I get a chance to study my reflection, I nod my appreciation. She's managed to keep my innocent look while adding a hint of sexiness, so different from the wanton look Michael wanted me to have at all times.

But, still the look of my enormous boobs won't stop bothering me. It's actually hard to notice anything else about me other than them. That's why I select a long black cardigan out of my wardrobe despite Lindsay's alarmed warnings against it. "You're gonna ruin a perfectly good dress."

"Just in case," I say and fill the black clutch she picked out for me with my phone, wallet, and keys.

"In case what? In case Zane notices what a hot chick you are?"

Smiling, I steal one last glimpse of my reflection. "I wish."

Sliding into the pumps, I tuck the clutch and the cardigan under my arm and head straight for the front door with Lindsay behind me. "Thanks for your help."

Outside, she wishes me good luck and gets into her car, waving at me as she drives out of the parking lot. My nerves won't give me a break as I start my car and head to the bakery on my way to Scarlet's party.

Zane likes a wide spectrum of women, but all have one thing in common, undeniable sensuality. I should suck up my fears and become the woman who'll turn him on, because my entire plan is doomed to fail if I can't create a physical attraction between us. Michael is six feet under and can't force me to blow his associates anymore. I won't be sexually abused. I should let go of my fears and focus on my mission.

Still, I just can't decide about the cardigan. When I pull up in front of the bakery, I give it a long, hesitant look, then decide to leave it where it is, on the passenger seat of my car. Suddenly cheerful with my determination, I get out of my car and head for the bakery.

Despite its small size, the bakery serves thousands of customers and has a wide reputation for its delicious cakes. A young girl is attending two women at one register with a catalog of cakes in her hands and from what I understand, she's showing them the wedding cakes they design and bake.

I eye the younger of the two women with curiosity. She must be engaged and planning her wedding. She looks to be in her late twenties, just like me, and radiates happiness. She must have found the love of her life to sport that kind of ecstatic expression.

A pang of jealousy hits me hard, like a fist right in my gut, making me wonder if I'll ever have anything romantic with Zane, much less marry him.

A young girl shows up at the other register, asks me for my order number, and disappears into the kitchen to get Scarlet's birthday cake. The front door opens with a jingle and a tall, dark-skinned man walks in. He glances at the two women at the other register and then strolls to one of the tables on my right.

I shift in my place, uncomfortable by the presence of a man, although he's neither talking to me nor interacting with me in any way, but I can feel his gaze on me. My cheeks turn hotter by the second, the muscles in my legs tightening. Breathing deeply, I glance around nonchalantly to calm myself, mentally whispering to myself that even if he's staring at me, it's just a harmless gesture.

From the corner of my eye, I can see the man shrugging out of his jacket and hanging it on a chair in slow motion. Curious, I crane my head in his direction and notice his face is turned to me. Not just that, he's ogling at me without a hint of shame, his eyes dark and hungry and sliding down my body. I still; air rushes out of my lungs as hurtful memories swim to the surface and the sickening leers of the men I had to please appear right before my face.

Michael might be gone, but depraved men are everywhere, and I'm exposing myself to them with inappropriate clothes that reveal my body to their wicked eyes.

As soon as the bakery girl comes back with the cake, I hurry out and into my car and slide on my cardigan. Tears sting my eyes. I quickly blink several times to prevent my makeup from getting ruined. The last thing I need right now is raccoon eyes.

I cover my torso with the cardigan nonetheless and cross my arms across my chest, unconsciously leaning back and forth, while the hurtful memories play in my mind with sordid details.

CH 15 - JULIE - The Shock

My phone rings in my bag with a text, startling me, reminding me of the little time I have left before I'll ruin the party.

The text is from Scarlet. She's so sweet, she's not complaining about my unusual tardiness, but letting me know that no one has arrived yet. Checking my makeup through the rearview mirror, I apply a fresh layer of my dark-pink gloss and start the engine.

Scarlet meets me at the entrance of her apartment building and grabs the box of cake. "Thank you for saving me the trouble. I've been cooking since the crack of the dawn and even so, the food isn't ready yet."

"Is there anything I can do to help?" I push the elevator button and straighten my dress and cardigan.

My move catches her attention, and dismissing my question, she smiles. "Oh, my God! Julie, look at you. You look lovely."

I wave at her and mirror her smile, trying to contain the thrill of being flattered, albeit by a girl, although I'm aware it's beyond silly of me. What am I, fifteen, needing confirmation of my appearance from a female peer?

"I had a simple menu," she begins when we step into the elevator. "Some finger food, and a salad and soup bar. That should be enough, right? Apparently not! Grannie didn't even let me finish when I mentioned finger food. Mom threatened to disown me. I know she was joking, but a salad bar is apparently an insult to them." She recounts to me the full list of food she had to cook. It seems we have a feast coming up. I feel glad for having skipped eating cookies.

Her mother and grandmother are just like Scarlet, and welcome me with sincere hospitality, hugging me and slipping me a large plate filled with samples of the food we're going to be served during the party. Then, they all excuse themselves to go change.

While nibbling the delicious food, I open the fridge doors and glance around in it to find a place big enough for the birthday cake. When I hear a knock on the front door, I quickly push the box onto the top shelf and run to get the door.

Zane stands at the doorway with his bedroom eyes bright and his lips curled up into a mischievous smile. He's wearing a brown leather jacket, blue shirt, and jeans that have me drooling for him on the spot.

"Hey, there!" He ruffles my hair and walks into the condo, while inspecting the living room space. "Where's everyone?" He turns to me and slips his hands into the side-pockets of his jeans, looking like a model with his bulging muscles. He's stunning, and my knees are starting to wobble.

"Scarlet and her mom and grandma will be back in a minute. They're changing. Her brothers must be out somewhere." I walk up to him in the hope that he'll study me as intently as he did at my condo, cursing myself for having buttoned the cardigan from top to bottom. Unbuttoning it now would be absurd and raise eyebrows at my insanity rather than my good looks, if I have any.

Still, my makeup is different than usual, more sensual and playful, and my hair is down around my shoulders. I should have enough appeal to attract his attention to me, right?

Apparently, no. Zane's otherwise inquisitive eyes land on the cream-colored leather couch before he leisurely strolls toward it, without so much as looking at my face. Shrugging out of his jacket, he lays it on the armrest and settles in the middle of the couch, his long arms spread on the back of the couch. "Nice condo, comfortable couch."

It hurts me how sexy he looks without even trying.

"Yeah, she has good taste." I move toward the armchair right across from him and stand for a moment before sitting to give him a chance to take a look at my body. He doesn't look and instead continues assessing the room. I come close to yelling at him to stop gazing at the nonliving objects when I, a very much living being, need those beautiful eyes of his on me, preferably at all times.

"You look good," I say, the words I'd rather him say to me. "I mean, you sounded very disappointed on the phone." Giving up, I sit on the armchair that pulls me in, making sure nothing of my body is seen. I should have checked my horoscope today, at least I'd have had a heads-up about the bad luck that seems to be my destiny today.

"I don't know." He shrugs. Dark and distant, his eyes wander across the room. "I think I'm done with dating. It's not working."

"What?" I shake my head vigorously. "You only had two bad dates. That's just the beginning. No one said you'd find your future wife immediately."

Finally, he turns his face to me but to shoot me an indifferent glance. "It's really not for me. I'm not made for marriage. I guess I'll go Ricky Martin's way and pay a woman to bear my kids. I'll have her sign a contract to release all her parental rights to me, but I'll keep her around to take care of the kids. It worked well for Ricky. With the right girl, why shouldn't it work for me, too?"

"What? You're going to hire the mother of your kids?" I'm not the only one who's insane, but somehow that thought isn't calming.

He shrugs and nods. "Yeah. It's the best solution."

"Your kids deserve a loving family, not a contractual relationship."

"Marriage is a contractual relationship, too. Besides, don't fifty percent of marriages end in divorce? It's impractical to tie all my chances to just one woman." He tries to sound uncaring, but I can hear the disappointment in his voice. Something else must be bothering him. Have I led him to believe he's not worthy of a woman's love and commitment by ruining his date with Ashley?

"You're gonna regret it. Your children will resent you for buying their mother." It's actually me who's regretful...for manipulating him. He might be a self-indulgent womanizer, but he's a good man and doesn't deserve to be robbed of his self-confidence.

A knock on the door comes to my rescue, because I don't have anything else to tell him, much less to give him a reason to continue with my manipulative plan.

When I stand to get the door, the sound of giggles from upstairs makes me turn my head to the three ladies walking down the stairs in beautiful and elegant dresses. Wow. My jaw drops at the bright colors—pink, red, and purple.

The front door shakes with a loud banging. "Scarlet, open the door."

"That must be one of my seven impatient brothers," Scarlet says with a slight shake of disapproval of her head, looking absolutely beautiful in her pink dress, the way I should have looked in mine, but contrary to me, she's proudly presenting her lean body without any interference of a baggy cardigan.

I hurry to open the door and exactly seven tall, blond, and well-built men stroll into the living room. I'm a woman in love with another man, but these guests are so hot, I can't stop my eyes from growing large and roaming up and down their bodies.

"Hey!" They line up to shake hands and introduce themselves to me, then to Zane. Joshua, Jason, Joseph, Justin, Jonathan,

Jeremy. I guess their parents ran out of names that start with J, because the last one, also the youngest, is Benjamin. They at least managed to scoop a J in the middle.

"We heard someone is aging today," Justin, the oldest, I assume, says cringing his face dramatically.

"Yeah, I don't know what there is to celebrate about hitting the wall soon," Jason comments with a loud laugh.

Confused, I glance at them, blinking heavily. "She's only turning twenty-three. That's hardly hitting the wall?" Whatever wall they're talking about, I must have hit it long ago and even torn it down with my twenty-nine years on earth, according to their definition.

"Don't listen to my brothers. They're being silly, as always." Scarlet comes and punches playfully against Jason's arm. "You're embarrassing me in front of my bosses."

Scarlet's mother and grandmother approach and help her scatter the boys with commanding hand gestures. The boys comply and head to the kitchen.

Taking advantage of the sudden silence that comes with the disappearance of the boys, Zane walks toward Scarlet's grandmother and grabs her hand gently. "Please tell me if you're Scarlet's mother or her aunt, because I'm perplexed by the striking resemblance." Lifting her hand, he brushes her knuckles with his lips until the old lady squirms with joy.

"I'm Margaret, and grandmother would be right." She corrects him while giggling like a school girl. That's what Zane does to women, no matter what their age.

"That is impossible." Zane shakes his head in disbelief, his beautiful eyes large and unbelieving.

"It's true, my dear." Turning to Scarlet's mother, she introduces her. "And this is my daughter, Helen."

Letting Margaret's hand go, Zane reaches for Helen's. "Pleasure to meet you. I assume you adopted those seven cowboys."

Helen laughs with an absolute pleasure echoing in her voice. "I wish." She lets Zane kiss her hand and then heads for the kitchen along with Margaret and Scarlet.

Zane gapes after them. "This is unreal. They say, check out her mother before marrying a girl to see how she'll look in twenty, thirty years down the road. But, this? That's the hottest grannie I've ever seen. Sizzling. Wow...just wow."

No one claims otherwise, but it's strange Zane points that out, especially the part about marriage. Is he considering Scarlet that way? I've never given it a thought, since Scarlet is so very young and the most important employee in the biggest show of his life so far.

"She's working for you," I indicate with a rather obvious tone of alarm in my voice.

He cranes his head and glances at me sideways without saying a word, the twitch of his lips telling everything about his thoughts. He likes her. He finds her attractive. He wouldn't waste a second to jump at her if the circumstances allowed.

My heart splits in two. Has he been attracted to her all along? While I was plotting ways to get his attention? I feel sick to my stomach.

His hands in his pockets, he starts

walking toward the kitchen to join the crowd and perhaps to gain the heart of the young, innocent girl he likes.

A tear runs down my cheek. Zane has been my focus of attention, the one person who monopolized most of my thoughts for so long, I fear for the future ahead. It's freeing on one hand. On the other, it's very lonely. He's my only family. Chloe and Ace are locked in their own worlds and barely have time for me. And, I've been in love with Zane for longer than I can remember. I can't just rip away my feelings for him and pretend I haven't been practically living with him in my mind twenty-four/seven.

That's why I shouldn't throw in the towel yet. Not without a decent fight.

A knock on the front door has me quickly reaching for my face and drying my cheek, and I hurry to get it. The four main male actors of Frat House show up with large gift boxes and bouquets of flowers. They're all insanely good-looking and also very sweet guys. Once again, I'm baffled by Zane's instincts in choosing such a crew of wonderful and dedicated actors who are also breathtakingly handsome.

"Come on in," I say cheerfully and open the door, standing beside it to let them in.

They give me hugs and then one by one disappear into the kitchen, where from the sound of it, the party is taking place. Scarlet talked of a small party, so I guess no one else is coming. I'm surprised Brad isn't invited. The director of the show is losing fans with his recent I'm-the-king-of-Hollywood attitude after adding the Emmy award for best director to his portfolio.

I draw a long breath to shake away the feeling of discomfort. When my muscles refuse to relax, I head for the bathroom and pat my forehead and neck with a washcloth soaked in cold water, glancing at my reflection.

It's not the first time Zane has shown interest in another female and it won't be the last unless I take control of the reins. Scarlet is a great girl, no doubt about it. In fact she's a perfect girl all around, but it doesn't mean she'll be the perfect fit for Zane.

Zane is a man of flaws. His flaws can actually fill a football field. Loving him means accepting him with all his imperfections. I can do that. I already do that. I go to bed, thinking of him, and open my eyes wondering how he's doing. He'll eventually see the truth by himself. I don't intend to force myself on him. But, I'll make sure he won't have to mold into someone that he's not, just to appease a woman who doesn't get him.

Drying my skin and applying a fresh coat of gloss to my lips, I leave the bathroom and walk to the kitchen. Two more guests have arrived, both from the crew, Scarlet's makeup artist and stylist, and they're joyfully chatting with Scarlet's brothers.

My eyes look for Zane in the crowd, and when I finally find him, talking with Scarlet's grandmother, he turns his head to wink at me. I can't help my insides melting at his gesture. Scarlet starts carrying plates and silverware to the dining room and I hurry to lend her a helping hand, grabbing the trays of finger food. Benjamin, the youngest of the brothers, snaps up more trays and helps Scarlet set the table with a practiced ease.

The guests surround the table and attack

the delicious food. I resist my urges and take only small samples of the food while conversing with Nick, one of the lead male actors in the show, and Chelsea the makeup artist, while occasionally exchanging glances with Zane. Every time my eyes look for him, he responds to my search with a sensual twitch of his lips and a rueful frown of his eyebrows.

Finally, someone switches off the lights, and Grandma Margaret walks into the dining room with the birthday cake decorated with two candles in the shapes of 2 and 3. Zane starts the Happy Birthday song and everyone quickly joins in, creating a loud choir under Scarlet's joyful gaze. She looks like she can hardly contain herself from jumping up and down, and as soon as the song ends, she blows out the candles with the sheer joy of a young child.

"Make a wish," her mother calls out.

Scarlet closes her eyes for a brief moment, her hands laced before her mouth as she makes her wish. Everyone claps hands and cheers. When she opens her eyes, with a huge grin, she lands them on no one other than Zane, who's standing right across from her on the other side of the dining table. I don't miss the intense longing and the deep penetration in her gaze, which has me frowning with fear and worry in a heartbeat, because Zane is reciprocating her gaze with an equal directness.

Then, she picks up a glass of champagne, holding it up and toward Zane. "I'd like to make a toast before cutting the cake." Her words draw cheers and more claps from the guests while I stand frozen, my eyes glued to the unmistakable exchange of glances between Scarlet and Zane.

Scarlet begins when everyone else grabs a glass of champagne off the table. "I'm an insanely lucky girl. Exactly eight years ago, on my fifteenth birthday, my biggest wish was getting accepted to the State University for a nursing degree. I'd then find a job at the local hospital and have a safe and stable life. That was my dream." Her voice falters and she pauses, rubbing her lips while filling her lungs with fresh air. "Then, my life changed into something I wouldn't even have wished in my wildest dreams. I was given a chance to be more than what I could have ever imagined. I have many people to thank for that, but only one person that'll have my undying gratitude for making Scarlet Landford a household name, and it's you, Zane." She lifts her glass higher, to reveal a large smile. "I would never have been here if you hadn't picked me for the role. I'll never forget your kindness."

My stomach churns as the realization of losing Zane hits me like a heavy blow. I'm losing him.

Zane rounds the large dining table between them and holds out his hand to Scarlet, and Scarlet catches his in the air, her face lit up and her eyes sparkling with an ecstatic look.

"If anything," Zane responds. "You are the one who made Frat House what it is today."

I'm going to throw up at the unusually charged exchange between the man I love and the girl any man would risk dying for while they hold hands. Then, fortunately, Zane pulls his hand away, and Scarlet picks up the knife and starts cutting the cake.

The worst thing is, I can't even be mad at this girl. If it were any other woman, I'd start hatching plans to get rid of her, but Scarlet? She's not only vital to Frat House, she's really a good and kind girl with practically no malice or hidden agenda beneath her glossy personality. I've met enough people to know she is who she seems to be without any pretensions.

But, it doesn't mean I won't act. I still have a shot at this. I won't give up before giving my last breath in this war of love. I only have to step up my game. And for that, I need to lose my fears, the first of which is my anxiety over being sexually objectified by men. And that means getting rid of my cardigan.

I excuse myself and disappear into the bathroom. My heart is beating fast, my stomach filled with flutters as I slide out of the cardigan and admire the beautiful dress once it's not shielded by my cardigan. Zane should have seen me this way when he first walked into the party. He's only a man and wouldn't remain unaffected by the sensuality the dress adds to my looks.

How strange it is that I yearn for him to gaze at me like the man in the bakery earlier, while that man's hungry look did nothing but scare the hell out of me.

With a deep breath of air, I hang the cardigan on the back of the door and step out of the bathroom. I return to the party, standing on shaky legs, but thankfully no one notices my wobbly steps.

My weary eyes scan the living room, my heart thudding unsteadily against my chest, my breathing shallow and irregular.

Zane isn't here. If he's left without saying goodbye to me, or seeing my updated self in my cute dress, all this stress will have been in vain. Just when the sinking feeling starts swirling around me like a tight robe, I hear his voice, very quiet, but still noticeable, coming from down the hall.

Nick approaches me right at that moment, holding up a glass of dessert wine. "Where were you hiding?" he asks, his gaze gliding over my body ever so slowly.

My hands fist in response, but I work hard to resist the urge to cover my chest. He's a friend, I keep telling myself in my mind.

I've known him for several years and he saw me in really sexual and revealing dresses when Michael was alive and forced me to look sexy for his clients. Nick didn't misbehave or in any way make me feel uncomfortable in his presence then. He's not like the men who took advantage of my circumstances. There're men who wouldn't rape a woman even if she's buck naked before them, and others who would attack a properly dressed women. And Nick definitely belongs to the former group of decent men. Besides, his appreciative gaze is actually an affirmation of the loveliness of the dress.

"Would you excuse me for a second?" I ask with an apologetic smile. "I think I forgot my purse in the bathroom."

"If you promise to come back to me afterward. I have something important to discuss with you." He nods and lifts the beautiful glass filled with sparkling red wine toward me.

I turn around and head for the hall, my ears on high alert for Zane's voice. Muffled sounds come from a room at the end of the hall. I slow my pace to even out the click of my high heels against the hardwood floor as I walk toward the room where Zane must be. Then I stop and listen because Zane isn't alone in the room.

He's with a woman.

Scarlet.

First, I can't make out anything of their conversation. That's why I lean closer to the door despite the major risk of being caught by them or the guests or both. It seems Scarlet is the only one talking right now. When I hold my breath and stay put, I can clearly hear her words.

"I've been waiting for a long time for the chance to have you all to myself," she says, her voice clearly tender and layered with affection.

The door is only a little ajar, keeping me from taking a peek at them. For all I know, she's in his arms, and that visualization cuts deeper into my heart than a butcher's knife.

"I know exactly what you are thinking of me. That I am too young and I won't be able to handle my emotions if we start seeing each other besides at work," she continues.

My lungs will burst if I don't fill them in

with a fresh breath of air, but I hold my posture, not moving a millimeter in order to hear the secret conversation taking place behind the door. I hear footsteps, high heels on hardwood floor, Scarlett's, specifically, along with soft breathing. The two must have been so engrossed with each other they didn't hear the sound of my own shoes as I approached the door.

"But, you're wrong," she whispers. "I can and I will keep myself in check, no matter what and be professional even if things don't work out."

Zane clears his throat but doesn't say a word in response to Scarlet's confession. My mind plays tricks on me and presents me with the image of Zane glancing at Scarlet with lustful eyes. I swallow the hard lump of frustration blocking my throat and allow myself to take a breath.

"You're a great girl," finally Zane starts. "You're incredibly talented and impressive in everything you do. And, and, well, you're breathtaking too, but you must hear that from other men every day of your life."

I hear Scarlet giggle and imagine her

blushing at Zane's compliment. I bet she looks astoundingly adorable with her cheeks all red.

"It's just... Frat House is my baby, and I don't want to be the reason for its failure. Getting involved with an actress is a foolproof recipe for that," Zane says.

"I totally understand your worries," Scarlet replies. "But, the same goes for me. Frat House is my life. I won't let my personal life influence it in any way. You know me. I haven't stopped being the hardworking, ambitious person that I was the first day on the set. I work hard every day so I won't fail at what's expected of me. I know how important the show is to hundreds of people. It's critical to me, too. It's what made me a famous actress. It's what gave me a career. My father passed away last year, and I was back at the set the next day after the funeral and worked my ass off without the loss of my father getting the best of me. I won't mess it up for anything. Even for you."

"In that case." Zane's voice comes through confident and clear. "I'd like to take you on a date. But before that..."

I don't hear anything for a long second, then Scarlet's soft breathy moan echoes in my ears along with the sound of lips tangling in a passionate kiss.

He's kissing her!

It's not the first time I've witnessed Zane with another woman, but this time, fear runs thick in my blood, and twines around my heart. I see danger blaring in my face in neon letters. I know it with every fiber of my being. I've lost my chance and she's going to win his heart.

My legs tremble, and I lose my balance and my hands land against the door to regain what little steadiness is left to me. The door opens as I launch toward it, but I manage to grab the doorknob at the last moment before hitting the floor face-first.

Wide with surprise, beautiful eyes glance at me. My tongue tied, I mumble, "Ahh..."

Zane untangles his beautiful girl from his body and runs to help me back up on unsteady legs, grabbing me by my arm. "Are you okay?" His touch on me doesn't spark an uncontrollable current through my body as it always has. Now it only feels distant and mechanical.

My eyes drift from him to Scarlet and I quickly nod my head. "Yes. I was looking for Scarlet." Shifting my pose to stand on both feet, I move away from Zane's touch. "I got a call from work. I need to leave now. Thanks for having me over. It's a great party. I love the food," I blubber mindlessly, grinning like a fool, my eyes carefully avoiding Zane.

"Of course. Thanks for bringing the cake." She walks toward me and wraps her arms around my shoulders, pulling me into a tight hug.

In a different world, she and I could be great friends, best friends even, but right now all I want is to circle my hands around her throat and take her last breath away. Which is why, I pull away quickly, unsure of what I'm capable of if I don't get a grip on myself.

"I'll see you guys later." I wave my hand in the air awkwardly and dash out of the room, wishing I could dash out of their lives as easily.

CH 16 - The Winner

Finally, the sun had turned her face my way and is shining on my life, warming me from inside out. And that sun has a name. Scarlet. She's not just a pretty face and a great body. She's everything I could wish to have in a woman and more...a humble personality, an unshakable work ethic, boundless love and affection, and a soothing smile. With her, I don't consider myself as a prize, since there can't be any bigger prize than her.

Even so, she spoils me with praise and attempts to convince me to give her a chance when it should be me who should be pursuing her. The irony doesn't even stop there. She takes hesitant steps toward me, her beautiful green irises glued to my lips, her hands splaying against my chest. The way she admires me makes me feel as though I'm some kind of Greek God.

The strapless dress is generously displaying her silky skin and the curvy tops of her breasts. And her flowery scent...just mind-blowing. Then she rises to her tiptoes in an effort to reach my lips when all I want and can think of is kissing her. The urgency is so strong, I can feel my lungs shutting down as the seconds pass before our mouths meet.

When she takes the last step and brushes her lips cautiously against mine, I can finally say I'm sold.

Raising her hands, she runs them through my hair and pulls me down harder against her mouth. The attraction I've been feeling toward her wasn't unshared. I had a suspicion of her interest in me but brushed it off as a platonic, friendly interest. The passionate kiss we're sharing proves to be anything but platonic. Her moves are so precise, yet tentative, I can tell she practiced this scene in her mind over and over again.

Running my hand up her back, I cup her

neck and press her toned body against mine a little too eagerly, the feel of her soft and sizable breasts against my chest pumping life into my cock. Rather than shying away from my aggressive move, she moans a soft sigh of pleasure and thrusts herself against my torso, molding herself to my body.

This time, it feels right without the slightest hint of doubt. She's the girl I've been longing to have at my side. She knows who I am and how I like to spend my free time. Well, how I used to at least, because that chapter of my life is over. I'm determined to become the man she deserves, although I'm not sure how I'll figure out how to tame my wild side because her body pressed against me is turning me wilder by the second. If she continues kissing me as if this is the last kiss she'll ever get, I might lose control and take her right here in this bedroom, only a few feet away from her entire family.

Fortunately, the door opens abruptly and Julie shows up, nearly tripping over Scarlet and me with her clumsiness. She must have a sixth sense or something for sensing when I'm about to get into trouble with my lack of control and have come to save me before I scare Scarlet away for good.

The thrill of having Scarlet when I couldn't even allow myself to think about the possibility of being with her is overwhelming and has me so lightheaded that I miss Julie's words. She's bubbling some niceties to Scarlet and then they hug.

It's impossible to look away from the goddess of beauty and loveliness before me. When I finally manage to tear my eyes away from Scarlet and land them on Julie, I note the shock tensing her facial muscles. It's more than the shock she's trying to hide over her embarrassment with her quick moves and fake smiles, although I can't put my finger on it. She's not angry like I expected her to be. I've known her long enough to read her face like an open book, but there's not a single clue to anger on her.

It's something else...something deeper, soul-ripping. I finally realize what, when she looks at me one last time. Fear, loneliness, despair...all wrapped up in a hurting glance before she excuses herself and steps out of the room, leaving me gaping after her.

THE END

DECEIVED

Forget me not: Part 1
by Liv Bennett

I'm dirt poor and unattractive, whereas Loraine is a beauty queen and wealthy enough to wipe her nose with hundred dollar bills every day. Yet, she wants me to seduce her husband and the father of her kids— Kenneth, the youngest and the sexiest self-made billionaire alive.

That she wants to divorce him to get most of his assets is a big fat lie and we both know it, because you don't just give up on a man like Kenneth, the very symbol of power and raw sexuality. You tie him down with chains and barb wires so he can't escape.

While searching for the real reason Loraine has hired me as a nanny, I'm working hard not to fall for Kenneth. That, too, proves to be a big fat lie.

~

Prologue

My hands grip the corners of the dryer in the laundry room, my body pressed against it per his order. The sweat-soaked, white, cotton t-shirt is the only thing I'm wearing and it's barely reaching the top of my bare buttocks. I tighten my fingers against the dryer to keep myself from pulling the hem of my t-shirt down.

My cheeks feel hot from humiliation and my mind wonders what he must be thinking.

"That ass..." he once said with an acute longing in his voice, the only time he referred to a part of my body. And even so, he didn't finish his sentence and kept me guessing about what he meant.

My knees tremble, and my feet turn colder the longer I stand on the marble floor. The floral scent of the detergent makes me feel nauseous and dizzy but not like the fear of the unknown.

I dare tilt my head, only a little bit, though, to see if he's still behind me, although I know there's no way in hell he'll forgive my last move and leave me be.

He's furious. He's always been for most of the time I've known him, but this time, anger is fuming out of his ears. He's murderous. Speechless. He's not even breathing. I can't foresee his next move. I'm not even sure how long has passed since he cornered me inside this claustrophobia-inducing tiny laundry room. Everything about his house is majestic, save for the laundry room where he has to confront me. My bad luck has always been an active and loyal participant in my life.

One minute I'm loading the washer with dirty clothes, the next minute he's shouting in my ear to take off my panties and bend over the dryer.

My mind is exhausted. I can't hold in my feelings any longer. I want to turn around to look at him, come clean about everything, and apologize for the depraved games I played with him.

I feel him move toward me, and my nipples harden against the soft fabric of my t-shirt. I want his hands all over my ass and his fingers to explore my sex, to turn this moment of humiliation into a wildfire of passion. I've been longing for him for so long; his mere presence has me drenched and aching for his touch.

But, he hasn't touched me. Ever. He's eye-fucked me countless times. He's yelled, threatened, and even openly told me to get out of his life before, but he has never laid a finger on my body, never made a physical contact.

Cold air hits my thighs, whereas hot flames are spreading between my legs. My heartbeats are loud against my chest, my breathing short. The waiting is killing me.

He takes another step behind me and suddenly his hand threads into my hair and yanks me back with a painful force. I scream in panic and sorrow. The first physical contact between him and me has to be this way?

I tremble and fall back against his hard torso that I've been dying to feel since the first time I met him. The rough surface of his jeans brushes against my buttocks, the warmth of his body turning up the heat inside me to an unbearable degree.

Panicked and fearful, I glance up at him and see his blue eyes flash with anger as they squint down at me.

"Did you seriously think you've got me figured out?" he whispers, each word radiating menace and revenge. "You think you know my weaknesses. You think I'll fall for your foolish games sooner or later." His hand pulls my hair more, forcing my head to press hard against his shoulder. "Don't you?"

Unsure of how to answer him, I groan to convey my pain and fear. My tongue wouldn't move anyway.

"Answer me!" he yells into my ear, and I wince in more pain. He'll murder me and bury my corpse in the woods. That's actually what he should do to fix the problem once and for all.

I scream again, hoping he'll see my fear and let me go. Instead, he shoves me against the dryer, my hips hitting hard against the sharp edge of the machine. His hand lands on my back between my shoulder blades and presses me down to keep me in place. An unnecessary move, since I wouldn't be able to run away anyway.

My nipples harden both in pain and pleasure. My thin t-shirt is rolled way up around my waist. And his hand is still on my back, slowly moving down toward my ass. My breath is caught up in my throat as the anticipation builds inside my chest. I can feel my sex swell and dampen for him, for his touch I'm pretty sure he'll deprive me of.

Nonetheless, his palm is now crossing from my t-shirt over to my bare skin. This is the very first time his skin has touched me. The thrill of finally feeling his heat and the hard planes of his body will make my heart explode. My clit throbs in hunger; desire is pulsating through my wet folds. I've been yearning for this moment and dreaming it every night.

My senses are heightened; my lips part to gasp for air.

He runs his finger down the crack of my ass. He grunts when his fingers slide between the moist lips of my sex, probing my tender flesh, his skin coated with my arousal. "Jesus!"

My mind turns foggy and my eyes close, the rest of my senses focused on only him. I still sharply when I feel his finger move further until it hits the tight knob of my clit. Even with my back turned against him and my eyes closed, I can sense his struggle as he circles the tip of his finger around my clit. Both of us know this will bring his end without a doubt, although neither of us can stop.

I wiggle my hips in rhythm with his moves, unable to stop the moans escaping my lips each time he presses the pad of his thumb against my clit, the heated pleasure of it making my eyes roll back in their sockets. The muscles inside my sex clench as the craving for release wraps around my body like a thick blanket. Sweat drops gather around my forehead. Each new second he keeps his hand between my legs is another step into insanity.

His finger moves back slightly, abandoning my trembling clit, and then suddenly dips into my wetness, rubbing the throbbing flesh inside my sex. With a moan, I push my ass against him, wanting him deeper and harder.

"You want me to rub your little cunt until you come, don't you? You need it so badly, you're ready to throw away your life for a momentary pleasure." He chuckles, clearly amused, then his voice turns stern when he says, "Some nights I go to bed with the thought of fucking you senseless driving me crazy. I can't sleep. I can't eat. I can't work. It's your doing, all of it."

I gasp and pant in desperation, as the friction of his finger inside me has me trembling with an agonizing need for release. Panic rises inside me when he stops his movements.

"Please, don't stop," I mumble, fearful of not being able to get the relief my body demands.

"Do you want it?"

"Oh, yes, please," I cry, my desire too great to contain.

As if my begging meant nothing, he yanks his finger out of me, cutting all the physical contact between us, and moves away.

"Do you honestly think you deserve my affection?" are the last words leaving his mouth, before I hear the door shut behind me.

Chapter 1

Present

The café is bustling with customers as usual for seven-thirty in the morning. Although Chris and I do our best, there's a long line of impatient customers waiting to get their morning fix of our house-roasted coffee.

My stomach rumbles as I place the order for the lady who's requested two sesame bagels with cream cheese and two muffins. I haven't eaten since lunch yesterday, and as it turns out nineteen hours on an empty stomach isn't the best condition for working as a barista. Drawing in a long breath of air to calm my raging stomach, I look up at the next customer with my practiced smile.

"Good morning. What can I get for..." My lips stop moving, and my jaw drops while I gape at the customer moving to the register.

I must have gone into a hunger-induced coma and be hallucinating the prettiest set of blue eyes I've ever seen. They're magnetic, sizzling and hold my gaze for longer than would be considered normal. Of course, the rest of the client's face matches up to the beauty of his eyes. Smooth skin flawlessly shaved, strong jaw, classical Roman nose, full lips that are twitching up at the corner in amusement. His masculine scent is pushing my mind into the unforgiving hands of euphoria and...suddenly I realize a significantly long moment must have passed since my coma started.

I blink my eyes several times and give my head a quick shake to dissolve the dream away and get back to my day. When I finally glance back at him again, the shock of seeing him hits me with the same strong blow. Perhaps due to seeing my confusion, he starts drinking me in as well, and as his eyes roam over my neck and chest, I feel my breathing falter and my heart race with excitement.

Chris calls the next customer to the cash register beside me, and I hear the lady in a nurse's uniform making tsk sounds in my direction before she gives her order to Chris. That's my clue to get back to my job.

"What can I get for you?" I mumble, tearing my gaze away from Mr. Magnetic Eyes' face, which seems to be the root of my imbalance. However, it's hard to escape his hypnotic pull because now my gaze is stuck on his exquisite suit that, I have no doubt, is hiding a trim athletic body.

He's very tall, easily six-feet-three, and when he moves toward the counter, he spreads his arms on both sides of the cash register, his gorgeous torso encompassing my entire view. A cold shiver runs down my spine. My stomach flutters at the sight of the endlessly wide shoulders and chest. It's a welcome change from all the embarrassing sounds of growling I've had to endure.

Despite the awkwardness of it all, I continue studying the only male who has managed to pull me away from the troubling thoughts of my constant hunger and the rent that's due in two days, the poverty I haven't been able to escape in my nineteen years. Which reminds me of the fact that I should pay attention to his order if I want to keep my eight-dollar-an-hour job with its shifts that prevent me from being able to work a second job to keep me afloat.

Magnetic Eyes' smile grows, and he places a twenty-dollar note next to the cash register. "A small cappuccino with four shots," he says. I guess he has realized my nonstop worship and is kind enough not to put me under the spotlight. "Keep the change," he adds.

That's sixteen dollars and fifty-one cents and for me two-weeks' worth of dinner money. I'm too poor to argue with him about his unusual generosity and give him my thanks with a soft voice while slipping the change into the back pocket of my jeans.

Chris takes over the next client while I prepare the order for Magnetic Eyes. Keeping my gaze fixed on the coffee machine, rather than on him, requires intense self-control. And of course I fail and allow my eyes to indulge in him one last time.

Jesus! He's so very hot, like Hollywood star hot, and I feel the room getting too warm. Just as I start admiring the details of his stunning features, the subtle shake of his head as if to say 'don't' makes me snap my attention back to the coffee machine just in time to keep from spilling cappuccino all over the floor.

He's wealthy and too handsome for the majority of women. I'm poor and so very ugly; I don't even have the right to look at him for longer than necessary.

Gulping down my disappointment and unending frustration with life, I place his cappuccino on the counter and call out his order loudly, although he's right behind the counter. I don't dare glance up at him when he says "thank you," but I don't miss the woman he walks out of the café with.

Of course, he's with a woman. What else would an overly hot and wealthy man walk around with? A Chihuahua?

Anger at myself for wasting my limited energy on unnecessary thoughts of a man floods my chest. I haven't eaten anything since lunch yesterday. If I don't calm my hunger soon, I'll pass out and possibly get very sick, and any illness right now will definitely cause me to wind up being homeless.

The unbearable hunger makes me come close to stopping a customer from throwing a half-eaten bagel in the trash, but I manage to control myself in the last second as I remember the sixteen unexpected dollars Magnetic Eyes left me with. I can have a full lunch with it. The only thing I have to work on is not passing out for the next three hours until my break.

Tom, the owner of the café, comes out of his office and crooks his finger at me to call me to his office. I nod and hurry toward him. "Did you need something?" I ask as cheerily as I can with my quickly diminishing energy level.

"Come on in." He walks into his office and closes the door when I follow him in.

With my heart up in my throat, I watch him settle behind his desk. Just yesterday, he fired a barista claiming she was embezzling, but we all knew it was his way of downsizing.

When he lifts his hand and starts scratching the back of his head, looking uncomfortable, I sense I'm the next to be laid off. It's a crappy job but it's the only café I can walk to from my home and not have to juggle busses. As it turns out, L.A. isn't exactly the place to live without a car, and I've never been able to save more than $200, which means I have to depend on buses and my feet for the foreseeable future.

"You don't look good. Is everything okay?" he asks.

"I'm fine. It's just...that time of the month." Where the only food my finances allows me to eat is peanut butter sandwiches.

"Oh, okay... Ahh, the reason I wanted to talk to you is that...the business has been very slow the last couple of months," he starts, and I feel lightheaded both with hunger and worry that I'm about to lose my job and have to look for something new. I'm one paycheck away from winding up on the streets, and if I have to look for another job, I might as well invest my last dollars into a quality sleeping bag.

"I won't be able to pay this month's paycheck on time," he adds.

I blink in confusion. I'm not the next downsizing victim? I never thought having a delay in receiving my salary would make me feel so relieved.

"Here's your paycheck for half your salary, and I'll pay the other half within two weeks."

I almost chuckle in happiness as I take the check from his hand and thank him before leaving his office. Despite Tom's claims about the slow business, more customers line up in front of the cash registers. Quickly, I pour a glass of water, gulping it down to calm my growling stomach, and return to the cash register.

"What can I get for you?" I ask with a smile and glance at the beautiful, tall, blonde lady before me. Is there a film shooting nearby? I mean, what's up with all these gorgeous and wealthy people invading our humble little café only nerds and elderly people normally frequent?

"Fifteen minutes of your time?" she says, intensifying my curiosity. "Oh, I'm sorry. I'm Loraine Carter. I'd like to have a little chat with you about a problem of mine if that's okay with you. I'll pay you for the time I'll be stealing you from your work."

Narrowing my eyes in suspicion, I study her black dress and Louise Vuitton handbag.

These wealthy people... They think they can get anything by mentioning money. "I can't take a break right now. Would you like something to drink?"

She pulls a wide red purse out of her expensive handbag and takes a fifty-dollar bill out of it, placing it with an unmatched elegance on the counter. "Could I please steal your colleague for fifteen minutes?" she asks to Chris, pushing the money toward him.

"Sure," Chris replies eagerly and takes the money. "Go ahead. I can handle the customers."

"Please," the lady in the black dress says softly to me, and I shrug and follow her to a table outside, wondering what kind of topic she wants to discuss with me that's worth fifty dollars.

"Thank you for agreeing to talk." She sits down on the chair gracefully, crossing her legs immediately, and places her handbag on the table. "I'll keep it brief for you."

I nod and settle into the chair, keeping my hands in the pockets of my apron. She has perfectly styled, light blonde hair reaching her shoulders, and bright green eyes. Her earrings and necklace are a thick set made of gold and probably cost a few thousand dollars, ditto for her black, body-hugging dress. Her skin is smooth, her makeup perfect as the rest of her appearance. What can such a perfect-looking and wealthy woman want to talk to a poor barista like me about? It's not like she loved the way I pour the coffee out of the coffee machine and now wants to have me as her personal coffee-pourer.

"I'd like to hire you as a nanny for my two kids," she starts.

"Excuse me?" Coffee-pourer would have been less awkward since she doesn't have a single idea about my child-care skills. For all she knows, I might be into child pornography and record her kids naked while bathing. Sick people are everywhere. That's why a responsible parent should run background checks and call a variety of references to make sure her kids are safe. I assume safety isn't on her priority list.

"Yes," she smiles and continues explaining with a gentle and friendly tone. "I need a nanny, but your main job won't be exactly looking after my kids. They go to daycare from eight 'til five and I'll be with them and with you the rest of the time. You won't really have to be their nanny in the real sense."

Her explanation makes me even more confused. "I don't understand."

"I need you to pretend to be my children's nanny, but your main duty will be...ahh, it'll sound very strange and I apologize for that, but... I'll need you to seduce my husband." Just when I start rolling my eyes, she leans forward and holds my elbow with a careful tug of her hand. "Please, don't go yet. Before you dismiss my proposal, it involves a lot of money. Like the kind of money that you won't have to work as a barista ever in your life again."

I swallow, curious and scared in equal amounts. She might be a Madame of a bordello on the lookout for her next virgin prostitute. Only I'm not a virgin and prostitution is really the last resort I'll consider and that is only if I face jail time for my debts.

"My husband is a very wealthy man," she

continues. "And I want to divorce him. But, because of our prenup, I'll most likely end up with a measly alimony and child support. I want half of his assets, and getting him to cheat on me is the only way I can get what I deserve."

I have serious doubts about her sight. Surely, it can't be as good as her looks if she's considering me appealing enough to seduce anyone, especially a rich man. She's a solid ten on the attractiveness scale, and I'd be probably five if I put on a revealing dress and get my hair done professionally. How can she expect me to seduce a husband who is used to her level of beauty? That is, if I were to accept her offer.

"Ma'am, thank you for considering me for the job you have in mind, but I'm an ordinary girl. I might be dirt poor, but I work my ass off so I don't end up sucking someone's dick off of the street. What you're offering me is exactly that. I won't become a whore to your husband no matter how much money you offer me."

"I'm so sorry. I didn't mean to offend you. Believe me, I love my husband and would remain married to him if it was up to me. But—" Her gaze falls on her hands on the table, and her lips begin trembling, signaling a sob that's coming any second. "—He's not the man I married. He's always been very attractive, and he's become very wealthy. But recently, he's become the center of attention since he appeared as the hottest five up-and-coming businessmen of the nation in a popular magazine. He's getting hundreds of love letters and emails every day from gorgeous women who are more than willing to become his whore for nothing. He probably wouldn't marry me if I met him now. I don't think he's cheating on me at the moment, but he's only human and will eventually succumb to his weakness. I don't want to be unprepared when he does. I want to control it when the worst case scenario happens. I want my husband to cheat on me with you so I have proof of his adultery and can use it against him in court."

She straightens up and looks right into my eyes. "I love him very much, but this suspicion and the fear that he'll leave me for another woman is killing me. I don't want to be hurt. And the only way to avoid it is having control of it."

She sounds genuine, and as silly as it may sound, I feel sorry for her. I take a long breath and glance up at her with a smile on my lips. "You don't know if your husband will find me attractive. In fact, I can assure you he won't even take a second look at me, if what you're saying is true about beautiful women throwing themselves at him. I'm not pretty." Hearing the truth about my looks from my own mouth makes my stomach churn in disgust. I don't have money. I don't have beauty in any sense. All I have is my drive to make it one more day in this ugly world without getting sick or having to beg someone else for food or shelter.

"You might not be beautiful in the traditional sense, but I witnessed earlier how my husband sized you up and down. The way he looked at you reminded me of the first time he laid eyes on me. It made me sad catching him eyeing a young girl as if he could fuck you right there and then, if the circumstances allowed. Believe me, I've seen him surrounded by women, but never once saw him glancing at any of them the way he looked at you."

She must have a different idea about her husband's attractiveness if he indeed looked at me for longer than half a second. I slip a hand out of my pocket and tug at the collar of my shirt in discomfort. "I don't feel good about the prospect of becoming someone's whore, a married man no less."

"Please, don't dismiss my offer just yet. Your help will mean a lot to me, and I'll reward you with a lot of money and other benefits. I have a wide network of friends, and if you want I can get you enrolled in a university of your preference, or get you a corporate job in addition to the money I'll pay you. Whatever you want, I promise you'll get it. And, if I didn't misinterpret the way you checked out my husband, you liked him, too."

"I'm not sure you saw it right. I don't check out customers. Ever."

"You do, my dear." She gets her phone out of her bag and pushes it up close to my face. I glance down at the screen and see in embarrassment the picture of her husband,

Magnetic Eyes, who tipped me sixteen dollar earlier. In my defense, my empty stomach and the shock of the offer had caused me to forget about the brief encounter with him.

"He'll give you the time of your life," Loraine continues. "I can assure you that. He's a sex god in bed."

"This is ridiculous. Sorry, but there's no way I can have sex with your husband, no matter how sexy he is." I push to my feet and start to head toward the entrance of the café. Chris must be already freaking out for having to attend the customers all by himself.

"Wait," she yells behind me, her voice loud enough to make my head turn. "Here. A thousand dollars in cash just so you think it over tonight."

My eyes land on the stash of money she drops on the table. A thousand dollars just like that? My goodness, how much money is she planning to pay me in exchange for my non-existent dick-sucking skills? Her offer might be an insult to my dignity, but I won't turn my back on money that basically requires nothing on my part. A thousand dollars means two months worry-free for me or finally buying a car and not being dependent on buses to get around in L.A.

"Deal." I nod, much too quickly, and walk back to the table to get the money before she realizes she's practically throwing it away.

She pushes the money toward me and then crosses her arms on her chest. "If you accept, I'll hire you for five months, and you'll get paid $4000 a month salary as a nanny. You'll receive it no matter what. But, if you can get my husband to sleep with you and have photos to prove it, I'll pay you another $200,000. I'll say it again, the $20,000 from the nanny job will be yours no matter what."

She's filthy rich but not very clever for not considering the possibility that I can basically attend her kids without even moving a finger to seduce her husband.

As if reading my mind, she adds, "You'll follow my plan verbatim to be able to keep your job for five months. The minute I notice negligence from your side, you'll find yourself out the door. That's my only condition."

I let out a long breath and grab the stash of money, glancing left and right to make sure none of my colleagues witness the transaction.

"This is my card." She places a business card on the table and gets up. "I'll be expecting your call by this time tomorrow. Don't make me wait too long."

"I won't." Slipping the card into the pocket of my apron along with the money, I watch her climb into a metallic-gray Mercedes parked in front of the café.

DECEIVED - Forget me not: Part 1 is available!

~

About the Author

Liv Bennett lives in California with her husband and daughter. Reading and writing erotic romance are her favorite forms of relaxation, in addition to long walks and yoga. She's a social drinker of coffee, but a serious tea addict.

Sign up to get alerts about her upcoming releases
eepurl.com/F_nqD

https://www.facebook.com/LivBennettAuthor (Please log into Facebook before clicking on this link)

slivbennett@gmail.com

Books by Liv Bennett

*

An Illicit Pursuit (Pat & Zachary)

*

Pursuit Series (Taylor & Adam)

*

Pleasure Extraordinaire Series (Lindsay)

*

Blinding Love Series

*

Fatal Seduction Series

*

Pleasure Extraordinaire Series (Zane)

*

Forget Me Not

Made in the USA
Lexington, KY
25 September 2017